Abuse of Process
Truth Wins

A. Author

Dedication

To our family, who all know He is the light of the world.

Acknowledgment

Thanks to those who impart love, joy, peace, patience, kindness, goodness, gentleness, and self-control. No thanks to those who are arrogant, rude, insist on their own way, irritable, resentful, rejoice at the wrong, and reject the truth.

About the Author

After spending over four decades navigating the complex world of banking and finance, the author emerges with startling truths to tell. "Abuse of Process," the first in a series of exposes that pull back the curtain on the troubling reality that a select few exercise immense power, using their influence and reaching into every crevice of not only banking and finance but politics and regulation too. This ensures their continued success at the cost of those who value honor and operate with integrity. Forced to choose between a lifetime of their retribution or silence, this family chose silence…..until now. Far from the luminous skyscrapers and bustling trading floors, they built a new life, a necessary sacrifice to protect themselves and their family.

The story, all names, characters, and incidents portrayed are fictitious. No identification with actual persons (living or deceased), places, buildings, and products is intended or should be inferred.

Preface

In the financial district of New York City, where the towering buildings witness the hustle and bustle of Wall Street, Graydon and Sophie forge their way, bound together by their purist dreams and resolute strength, to succeed in the business world.

As they celebrate their 10th anniversary and prepare to ring the opening bell at the New York Stock Exchange, little do they know that their world is about to be turned upside down. What begins as a joyous occasion soon spirals into a web of deceit and betrayal when a powerful banker steps in to crush their dreams. From starting his career as a bank teller to launching a financial ETF, Graydon Maxwell quickly achieves what few can dream of.

In this first of a series, the tale of their love and success is inscribed. Done so that history records that ordinary people can rise with the resilience and support of their loved ones.

Follow their adventures as they move forward, knowing that the existence of truth is above the omnipresence of lies.

This is a story of triumph over adversity, of love conquering all, and of the indomitable spirit of two individuals who refuse to be broken. A reminder that no matter how dark the night may seem, there is always light in the morning.

Contents

Chapter 1: The Bell Tolls for Thee

The sound reverberated in his ears as he looked at the hammer in his hand after ringing the bell. The New York Stock Exchange building stood as a resolute symbol of commerce and finance. Graydon Maxwell had stood outside the building for a few moments, allowing himself to quietly enjoy his success and, now, fulfillment of a dream. The very foundation of the position he had achieved was based on integrity and truth. He had envisioned this moment a million times in his head.

The evening before, as he took the first step out of the luxurious Mercedes, his eyes were blinded by the flashes of cameras as the mob of photographers and reporters clamored around the hotel's entrance. He tightened his hand around Sophie's, and she returned a gentle, reassuring squeeze as he helped her out of the limousine. He looked back at her, shielding his eyes from the flashes, and thought of how fortunate he was. Her beautiful dress, her determined composure, her strength.

They walked hand in hand as they made their way past the paparazzi to enter the hotel. The grand doorway had appeared so close but now seemed so far away as the pack moved into their path, chattering, "That's Graydon and Sophie Maxwell." One reporter asked, "Where are interest rates headed?" Another shouted, "Do you have any stock tips for us?" The probing reporters continued with more questions as they scribbled on their notepads. Graydon had been in this business long enough to know what was being recorded on those notepads: Gossip, rumors, and lies.

The Maxwells knew answering one question would lead to many others, so they graciously smiled and headed toward the steps. As Graydon moved forward, all he could think about was how fleeting these moments would be. He loosened his grip around Sophie's hand, and she locked her fingers with his, evoking thoughts of how he felt when he first saw her.

The Doorman greeted them with a warm smile, tipped his hat politely, and said, "Welcome to New York, Mr. and Mrs. Maxwell." As soon as they stepped into the hotel lobby, they felt a refreshing blast of cool air, and they both let out a deep sigh of relief, finally shielded from the outside world. The sounds of the city were muted as the gilded glass doors closed behind them.

Meanwhile, Sophie wondered where her husband's mind had gone. "What did you think of that?" she asked while poking Graydon in the ribs.

"I don't know what just happened. It was all a blur," Graydon chuckled.

"You're changing the financial industry, honey; you're making history. The public's attention comes with the job description," winked Sophie as she kissed him on the cheek.

Their sweet, intimate moment between was interrupted by a concierge who stepped up to them and, in a regal tone, said, "Good evening, Mr. and Mrs. Maxwell. Welcome to New York City. We trust you've had pleasant travels today. Your suite has been prepared with special amenities just for you and is ready for your arrival."

"S-suite?" Graydon asked with a puzzled look, "But we didn't reserve a suite."

The concierge chuckled to himself and said, "Your reputation precedes you, Mr. Maxwell. The suite and all the hotel's facilities are available to you 24/7 during your stay. We are honored to have you here with us." The staff did their job well and found out the identity of the Maxwells, which gave them time to arrange their finest accommodation. "What we don't know is what brings you here today, sir? Your guest file indicates you've stayed at several of our other properties over the years but not here."

"Firstly, we are gratified by your hospitality. And yes, we've stayed at many of your other properties and have always been beyond satisfied with their services. We are here to ring the New York Stock Exchange opening bell on Tuesday."

"Oh my! Congratulations!" the concierge replied. Another clerk, an older gentleman, stepped closer, smiled, and added, "That's a rare accomplishment worthy of note. Can we assist with transportation or any other preparations?"

"At the moment, I can't think of anything. I'm sure we will have a few questions tomorrow. I assume we should direct them to the Concierge desk?" Graydon asked while looking at both these clerks.

"Yes. If they don't answer promptly, then please call the Front Desk." he nodded as he stood next to the other clerk, conversing in hushed tones while he completed the check-in process. "Also, if you have not made dinner plans for this evening, may we suggest our Michelin Star restaurant? I'm happy to reserve a table for you and your lovely wife. If you'd prefer to stay in tonight, the room service menu is available twenty-four hours a day. Whichever you choose, I'm confident you'll be pleased as our Executive Chef and kitchen staff are recognized as one of the finest culinary teams in the city. Enjoy your stay." He smiled as he handed Graydon two key cards to their room.

"Thank you very much, sir. Looking forward to it." Graydon took the cards from his hand and turned around.

The clerk signaled a bellman who proceeded to take Maxwell's coats and luggage while smiling and quietly saying, "Onward to the Presidential suite." As the staff worked together with the coordination and efficiency of worker bees, Graydon and Sophie took in the luxurious surroundings. Stone arches and Greco-Roman pillars adorned the entire foyer, and beautifully scented flowers gave the air a fairytale-like quality. Marble tiles with silver and gold inlays adorned the walls and floors, glistening under the luminous crystal chandeliers. The lavish attention to every detail was breathtaking. They looked up and were amazed at what they saw; the ceilings were adorned with Renaissance-era murals.

Graydon had studied mythology in college, and it didn't take him long to recognize that the painting was Prometheus being chained by the Gods for giving fire to humanity. The art sent shivers down his spine as Prometheus's story was similar to his. He was bringing innovative financial ETFs to the markets, which could change them forever. After all, you don't expect or plan to enter the financial world, transform it, destroy a few empires, and build your own on top of the rubble without expecting repercussions.

Sophie called it paranoia, but he knew that their world was just as fragile as the ones he might topple. The fear of failure and the thought of going backward in life often haunted him. Once again, he seemed lost in his thoughts. Sophie's brows creased in worry, and she waved her hand in front of Graydon's face in good-natured fun, exclaiming, "Earth to Mr. Maxwell." Graydon shrugged and gathered his thoughts and once again calmed himself down. He knew if Sophie weren't with him, he might have to learn how to handle stress. He wouldn't be here without her, and he knew he'd choose her ahead of all the riches he could envision. Nothing was more priceless to him than his lovingly devoted wife. Theirs was a love made in Heaven; they both knew it the first time their eyes met.

Graydon's proverbial optimism and cheerful smile returned, and with his fingers still interlocked with Sophie's, they made their way to the elevator, which seemed luxurious on its own. As the elevator doors slid open, another hotel staff member appeared to escort them to their room. The doors closed as she scanned her lanyard and pushed the restricted button to the top floor. The young woman had a nervous excitement about her. She fidgeted and maintained a sly smile during the entire ascent to the top. The Maxwells looked at her curiously, wondering what reason there could have been for her peculiar behavior. Graydon thought she was likely a new hire, while Sophie imagined the young woman had just recently become engaged to the man of her dreams.

As the uncomfortable silence and fidgeting grew, Graydon started inspecting the surroundings and realized his thoughts as to technology advancing more rapidly in the near future were correct. From top to bottom, the elevator car had excessive decorative and technological features, from inlays of gold and other flourishes to small video screens near the top of the side and back walls, each on a different channel. Graydon chuckled to himself; after all, it was the new millennium. They were bound to see more video screens everywhere as the years progressed. Graydon had been one of the first to hear from some of his communication industry friends about mobile phones becoming 'smart' while at the same time, his technology contacts spoke of 'laptops,' with both becoming globally compatible. Though he had initially laughed at what he thought to be far-fetched ideas, he had come to learn that the world was always moving far quicker than he realized.

After what they felt was a rapid speed, they reached the top floor of the hotel. The young woman led them to the main doors of their suite and said, "Your luggage will be arriving within 15 minutes. Enjoy your evening, Mr. and Mrs. Maxwell." Sophie and Graydon thanked her for her hospitality, and as they turned around to unlock the door, she exclaimed, "Mr. Maxwell, a moment, please, sir."

"I apologize for appearing overzealous, but as a business major, I have followed your career with great interest. Honestly, I even decided to pursue a career in business because of your story, how you began from nothing," she exclaimed.

Feeling slightly flustered, Graydon replied, "Oh no, well, you're giving me much more credit than I deserve." Her admiration made him feel flattered but uncomfortable, too. His shy grin and nervous chuckle were proof of his honest humility.

The young lady was persistent. She described how her mother desperately wanted her to be a dentist and how she fought to study business after learning about Maxwell's success story. With enthusiasm, she revealed that she had applied to their investment firm for an internship only yesterday. "Please excuse me for not properly introducing myself. I'm Victoria Rossi, and I'm thrilled to meet you," she said in a gleeful tone.

Sophie and Graydon smiled at each other; the girl reminded them of themselves when they were much younger, hustling all the way to where they came now. Graydon scribbled his assistant's numbers on a hotel notepad. As he handed the piece of paper to Victoria, he told her that she was welcome to contact them at any time. He added that he looked forward to reviewing her application. She thanked him for his time and consideration and added, "It's been an honor to meet you, Mr. and Mrs. Maxwell. Have a wonderful evening!"

The Maxwells had experienced upgrades and perks at other properties but did not expect their key cards to have opened the door to more than a standard room. They smiled at each other with delight as the foyer, living room, dining area, and bedroom presented themselves. It was one of the most majestic rooms, with golden hues set against gradients of white. "I guess the older clerk heard or read about us and took note," Graydon remarked. "Well, of course, he's savvy enough to know this is where we'll return for our future visits to the Big Apple," Sophie exclaimed.

Sophie whistled and said, "We're not in Kansas anymore, Toto." Graydon smirked, and they held hands as they explored the huge suite. The furnishings were posh, like those seen in magazines like Architectural Digest, a far cry from those he grew up with. Hi-tech features were everywhere, and an advanced sound system filled the suite with soothing, smooth jazz tunes. In the living area, behind the grand piano, were sliding doors that opened to a huge balcony furnished with a French Bistro set and a small greenhouse filled with fragrant lavender, tea roses, and bougainvillea.

The dining room included a table large enough to seat twelve people comfortably. Flat-screened televisions with hundreds of films and stations to choose from could be found in nearly every room. The primary bedroom had a California king bed embellished with a dupioni silk duvet cover to coordinate with the fabric-covered walls. The adjoining bathroom was resplendent in glass, golden fixtures, and marble. Graydon and Sophie felt like they were experiencing life in another world.

Graydon became who he was not out of self-preservation but out of the fear that he wouldn't be able to give Sophie the life he felt she deserved. He knew staying in the Presidential suite in this five-star hotel wouldn't last forever. As long as he and Sophie had each other, they would have the riches many people search for their entire lives and never find.

Graydon kissed Sophie's forehead tenderly, "You deserve every bit of joy this world has to offer, Mrs. Maxwell." Sophie looked at him with loving admiration and replied, "Our love is my favorite joy."

They held each other quietly for a short while, listening to the soft jazz as it filled the room. The music created the perfect ambiance to wash away the stress and negative energies brought on by the hustle and bustle of the day. They realized it had been months since they had experienced such calmness together; they deserved to rest.

"Let's go with room service tonight," Graydon suggested.

"Perfect," Sophie replied.

They enjoyed a delectable dinner, including their favorite dessert. As they finished their crème' brulèe, the clock struck midnight. With a goodnight kiss, they closed their eyes and drifted away to dreams of what tomorrow's morning light will bring.

Chapter 2: The Sweet Chimes of Triumph

The sound of car, truck, and taxi horns filled the air as Graydon and Sophie stepped onto the busy Wall Street sidewalk. A thrilling electric experience suspended in midair, pulsating with the possibility of winning or losing fortunes. The structure, a National Historic Landmark and representation of the financial might of America, stood out against the backdrop of skyscrapers. With the warm glow of the morning sun, a magnificent blend of Greek Revival and Neoclassical architecture was illuminated. The facade was dominated by six enormous Corinthian columns, each taller than a four-story building. Crafted from white Vermont marble, they emanated sturdiness and power, an appropriate representation for the establishment they held. The pediment above them was adorned with elaborate sculptures that represented industry and trade. Capitalism as its foundation. It seemed to whisper stories of the economic triumphs over failures these walls had witnessed throughout history.

Sophie, her hair a golden halo in the sun, reached for Graydon's hand, her touch grounding him amidst the chaos. "It's incredible, isn't it?" she breathed, her voice filled with awe.

A proud American flag fluttered in the breeze atop the building, its stars and stripes vibrant against the clear blue sky. Below it, on the iconic balcony overlooking Broad Street, a crowd of well-dressed individuals had gathered. Their hushed voices and eager faces added to the atmosphere of anticipation. The heavy bronze doors leading into the Exchange gleamed like polished mirrors, reflecting the street's liveliness. As they stepped across the threshold, the splendor of the interior unfolded before them.

Soaring ceilings adorned with ornate plasterwork created a cathedral-like atmosphere. Rows of sleek, mahogany trading posts stretched across the vast marble floor, each one a mini battleground where fortunes were made and lost. The air thrummed with the low hum of conversations. Everything about the New York Stock Exchange, from its imposing exterior to its lively interior, spoke of competence, tradition, and the persistent quest for financial success. Yet, for Graydon, standing beside Sophie, their shared love and support, stronger than any financial empire, truly stood out in all its majesty.

Graydon squeezed her hand. "Indeed, it is, mi amore," he agreed, his voice thick with emotion. "But not as incredible as you are, standing here beside me." He turned to her, his eyes still reflecting the sunlight and the affection he felt for her. "I wouldn't be here without you, Sophie. You've been my rock, my confidante, my everything."

Sophie's smile bloomed. "We've built this together," she countered, her voice laced with faith. "Every single step. Remember those late nights, fueled by reheated leftovers and caffeine, poring over files and spreadsheets in that tiny apartment?"

A chuckle escaped Graydon's lips as the memory washed over him. "And the countless times you talked me up when I was on the ledge of self-doubt with your unwavering belief?" Their eyes met a silent conversation passing between them. They reminisced about the countless challenges they had overcome together, their partnership the cornerstone of their success.

"You're more than just my partner, Graydon," Sophie continued, her voice tender. "You're my best friend, my love, my sole source of happiness. I'm so proud of the man you've become."

Graydon pulled her into a tight embrace, his heart swelling with gratitude. He had conquered the concrete jungle with her by his side, and this momentous occasion was further glorified by the love he shared with Sophie. At that moment, surrounded by the symphony of the city and the weight of his achievement, all he truly desired was to share this victory with the woman who held his heart. As they parted, a hush fell over the gathered crowd. A stock exchange official approached them, a welcoming smile on his face. "Ready to ring the opening bell, Mr. Maxwell?"

Graydon looked at Sophie, his gaze filled with love and shared triumph. "More than ready," he declared, with a hand outstretched toward her. "Together."

"Great, please follow me," the official ushered the Maxwells toward their destination. On their way, he introduced himself, "I'm Tom Harvey, the Director of Public Relations at the NYSE." Graydon and Sophie followed him.

"It's a pleasure to meet you, Mr. Harvey. I'm Graydon Maxwell, and this is my wife, Sophie."

Tom's smile was warm and genuine, his eyes twinkling with an excitement that mirrored their own. "It's an honor to meet you both. Today marks a significant milestone, and we're thrilled to have you grace our podium."

"Thank you, Tom," Sophie replied, her voice brimming with nervous excitement. "We're incredibly grateful for this opportunity." Tom led them through the bustling throng, the air thick with anticipation and the low murmur of the exchange floor. Heads turned briefly as they passed, and whispers followed. "That must be the Maxwells!" someone said. "The ones ringing the bell today?" another asked. Graydon and Sophie exchanged a glance, a silent understanding passing between them. They were no longer just two individuals; they were ideals for youth, their journey culminating in this very moment.

As they entered a secluded area reserved for dignitaries, Tom continued, "Would you like a moment to prepare before we step onto the balcony?"

"We'd appreciate that," Graydon replied, his voice betraying a hint of adrenaline. He knew he was on the precipice of something historic, and the weight of the occasion pressed upon him.

Tom nodded and ushered them into a quiet, elegantly furnished room. They could see the expectant crowd below through large windows, their faces a sea of keenness. A sense of awe settled over them as they absorbed the enormity of the moment.

In that serene room, surrounded by the weight of history and the promise of the future, Graydon and Sophie found solace in each other's unwavering support. The opening bell rings to mark the start of the day's trading session, but for them, today, it marks a reward for their hard work.

After a few moments, Mr. Harvey returned, knocked quietly, opened the door gently, and said, "Mr. and Mrs. Maxwell?" In unison, the couple replied, "Yes, sir." The director gave a few instructions with a reminder to ring the bell as the clock struck at half past nine." Graydon took a deep breath, and Sophie held his hand tightly to show her support. They followed Mr. Harvey through a maze of corridors, revealing an inside glimpse behind the hustle and bustle of the trading floor. They felt very privileged, like VIPs with a backstage pass.

As Tom ushered Sophie and Graydon to the podium, a wave of emotions washed over them. The personal achievement was undeniable when looking back on years of toil and dedication fulfilling in this singular moment. Graydon's mind also drifted toward the broader significance, the impact that resonated beyond their journey.

Today's momentous occasion wasn't just about ringing the bell; it was about the story behind it. Their financial ETF (Exchange Traded Fund), a brainchild born from countless brainstorming sessions ruled by conviction, had carved a unique path in the financial landscape. It represented not just a profitable venture but a novel approach.

He glanced at Sophie, her hand firmly linked with his. Her blue eyes sparkled with pride, reflecting the heartfelt gratification that filled his. They had defied expectations, challenged the status quo, and emerged victorious. This bell ringing wasn't just a figurative event but a validation of their diligence and commitment to each other.

As they stepped onto the podium, the weight of the moment settled upon them. A hush descended over the traders on the floor below, their gazes fixed on the clock, waiting for the official signal to begin the day's trading. The weight of the gavel in Graydon's hand felt heavier than expected, not from the ornate silver and walnut handle, but from the weight of history created by a Wall Street outsider, a maverick about to gain a controlling stake in a venerable institution through his revolutionary ETF.

The clang of the opening bell, normally a signal for the start of the financial frenzy, transformed into a splendid carol today. The gaiety was mirrored as the merriment of a different kind. The chimed bell emulated with jingle bells, donning a Christmas-like cheer in the most capitalist area of the town. For Graydon, it was indeed a gift from above, an occasion that called for a celebration.

As he stood on the podium, the iconic NYSE floor stretched before him. A symphony of shouts, hand signals, and the rhythmic clinking of orders. But all he could see was Sophie, her eyes shimmering with delight, a silent echo of the countless late nights they had spent huddled over spreadsheets. *Together.* The word resonated within him, a mantra that had propelled them through every hurdle, every moment of doubt. This wasn't just his victory; it was theirs to share. This chapter of their love story wasn't simply about financial triumph. Most importantly, it was about their unwavering devotion to a lifelong partnership.

While their outward demeanors exuded a quiet confidence, internally, their hearts pounded as their minds grasped the enormity of these moments. Sophie worked to keep her steady, sanguine smile as Graydon concentrated on keeping his breathing steady. Yet, their intertwined hands, a silent proof of their shared journey, spoke volumes. These were the hands that had anchored each other through countless brainstorming sessions, the hands that had written countless lines of code, the hands that had built an empire, brick by digital brick. The couple had reached another zenith of their lives together.

They felt a curious blend of anticipation and awe as they stepped down from the platform to the trading floor, walking amongst the traders and staff. Off to the side, several bright lights highlighted the area where numerous financial reporting outlets were live on air. A floor reporter approached and asked several questions to which they carefully chose their words, knowing how stories can enter the hungry maw of the news cycle in a manner not intended.

They had been young, hungry, and desperately in love. Their apartment, though small, held a universe of possibilities. Every corner resonated with the harmony of their dreams, the clacking of keyboards as they strategized late into the night with a shared pizza. The floor served as their makeshift conference room, littered with crumpled papers and financial reports crafted purposefully to enlighten and inspire.

Sophie's finger traced the faint scar on his wrist, a remnant from a late-night mishap with a stapler, now a life-long reminder of the hectic and joyous pace of their life back then.

"Are you thinking what I'm thinking, darling?" she whispered, her voice tinged with laughter and fondness.

Graydon chuckled, "The time you accidentally set off the fire alarm trying to make instant ramen using oil instead of water at 1 A.M.?"

Gentle, genuine laughter filled their quiet space, contrasting with the roar of the trading floor. Each shared memory broadened their smiles further. They recalled the occasional arguments, fueled by frustration and exhaustion, but always resolved with a kiss and a renewed sense of purpose. They remembered the elation of Graydon's first breakthrough, a tiny spark that ignited a fire within them.

The small apartment, once a mark of their modest beginnings, had become a vessel, imitating their resilience and firm belief in each other. Graydon had emerged not just as a successful entrepreneur but as someone who had entered his name in the Book of Fame in golden words.

They walked outside and were bathed in the sun's soft glow. The brilliance of the NYSE fell behind as they walked down the block hand-in-hand to the Mercedes sedan. "We'd like to see Times Square and stop by Central Park," Graydon said to their driver. "Might as well take it all in," he said with a relaxed smile.

Chapter 3: Origins of Ambition

The math is simple. Think of it this way: if someone pays 100 for a 2% coupon that matures in one year, their yield will be 2%. If they paid 101, their yield drops to 1% because they have amortized, which is an expense, the 1-point premium. Conversely, if they paid 99, their yield rises to 3% because they accrete, which is income, the 1-point discount. Amortize and accrete, two words from the financial world, now made perfect sense to Graydon as he sat in his first Financial Concepts class.

FC class was a requirement for sophomores at Grove High, a four-year school with more than 2,000 students, and it was here that he began to recognize that he comprehended information on an intellectual level beyond that of most of his classmates. He started developing a vast understanding of finance, an unusual focus for a boy his age.

His parents had repeatedly imparted, "Just blend in and stay out of trouble, young man." A reflection of how they lived. Their 24-seat diner on Greenwood Avenue, a few blocks from Main Street, blended in with the buildings on either side. They were open from 6:00 a.m. to 6:00 p.m. on Monday – Friday, with a limited menu featuring natural ingredients prepared and presented simply and straightforwardly. Their hard work, combined with prudent spending, provided Graydon and his younger sister, Ida, with comfortable lives boosted by the knowledge that customers appreciated and respected their parents.

Saturdays were spent on household and yard chores. The scent of freshly baked seasonal cakes or pies would mingle with a broom's rhythmic swish and a hammer's distant thud. Graydon's father worked hard in the backyard and around the house, finishing the tough jobs and leaving Graydon with what he thought he could handle. His sister was not as eager to comply with her required chores; nonetheless, she completed them with a cheerful attitude. Both were now old enough to be assigned kitchen duty for lunch and dinner and closely followed the recipes laid out on the counter.

Graydon and Ida did not complain about their weekend responsibilities. Working together on Saturdays was a badge of honor, demonstrating the family's strong work ethic. While their friends might be off on a weekend adventure, they reveled in the tangible satisfaction of jobs well done.

A typical Saturday in the summer would start with dusting, then sweeping, followed by the whir of the vacuum. Next came the battle with the overflowing laundry basket as each shirt, skirt, and pair of pants was washed, dried, and folded or hung with precision. Next came the outside with the recurring click-clack of the lawnmower, leaving behind a green canvas for meticulous edging and sidewalks to be swept.

Any spare time would be devoted to helping neighbors. Next door, during the Summer, Mrs. Bale would need help trimming her overgrown hedges, which earned a warm smile and a plate of her legendary chocolate chip cookies. Each Spring and Fall, further down the block, Mr. Adams had become too frail to turn over his garden. While they worked the soil, he would tell stories of his life experiences and, when finished, would gift them an old hard-cover book he had on a subject they had discussed.

By the time the Sun dipped below the horizon, a deep sense of accomplishment would settle on Graydon and Ida. the knowledge that they contributed and made a difference, however small. It wasn't just about chores; it was about the values instilled through them. The value of hard work, community, and finding joy in the simplest things. Their parents believed these seeds would one day blossom inside them and lead to success that would be measured not just in financial terms but in the quiet satisfaction of a life well-lived.

Sunday morning began with the aroma of freshly baked cinnamon rolls, which motivated Graydon to get out of bed and put on a crisp button-up shirt and dress pants. He always noticed the neighborhood was quieter, which enabled all the birds to be heard.

As they walked toward the church, they would hear the soft chime of the tower bell. Sunlight dappled through the leaves of century-old oak trees, casting light and shadows on the sidewalks. Inside was a familiar smell of candles burning and polished wood. The warm glow of stained-glass windows bathed the parishioners in kaleidoscopic images. Graydon and his sister took their usual spot in the pew next to their parents, his gaze falling upon the worn wooden cross at the altar. The familiar words of the hymns would resonate through the church, sung with a mix of veneration and joyful devotion.

However, the church wasn't just about hymns, prayers, or sermons for Graydon. It was also a social space where he could catch up with his friends after the service. They'd share stories about their weeks, chuckling over shared experiences and individual exploits while knowing they were still under their parents' watchful eyes.

Once a month, everyone would gather in the church's fellowship hall for a potluck lunch, a feast of flavors brought together by the community. Graydon and Ida would eagerly devour Mrs. Hernandez's spicy empanadas and Mr. Vito's spicy meatballs, a testimony to the cultural diversity in their neighborhood. Following an afternoon filled with good food and fellowship, Graydon would walk away with a true sense of peace and belonging. Church was more than just a religious duty; it was a cornerstone of his community, a special place where he felt connected to something larger than himself.

The other Sundays meant the family looked forward to the scent of a slow-cooked roast lingering in the air as they returned from church. After a hearty meal, a sense of calm descended upon the Maxwell household, enhanced by the occasional rustle of turning pages and the gentle hum of the ceiling fan.

Graydon settled down on the living room rug with a well-worn copy of "Business and Finance" in his hands. The tattered cover, adorned with a faded print, promised an afternoon of learning. After his leisurely reading, he was required to complete his homework for the next day. His sister, however, would escape into the fantastical world of her storybooks about princesses, knights, and castles. Graydon, with his keen interest in business literature, could never relate to her aesthetics. "You are so delusional to believe in these folklores, silly!" He teased. His taunting would irritate Ida so much that she would pop off, requiring their mother to become the referee in their spats. At the end of the day, their sibling bond was unbreakable, and they always had each other's backs.

When she wasn't busy cooking, cleaning, or playing referee, their mom favored being curled up in her favorite armchair, and a well-loved Jane Austen novel opened on her lap. She drifted away to the world of witty heroines and grand ballrooms, far removed from the demands of her daily tasks. Relaxing in his recliner, the senior Mr. Maxwell would peruse the local newspaper. After reading the headlines, he was mostly interested in the local weather forecast and the food editor's restaurant reviews. He would often discover and clip new recipes to test at their cozy café. His focus was momentarily interrupted as he glanced at his peaceful wife and contented children. A smiling countenance revealed his profound gratitude for the gift of such a wonderful family.

Following a stroll through the nearby park, the family ended their favorite day of the week with a board game and a heaping bowl of popcorn. Graydon was tough to beat at Monopoly, while Ida, even though she was the youngest, was the Scrabble champion. Regardless of the scores, their parents always felt like winners because they believed nothing was more rewarding than spending family time together.

On school days, Graydon always looked forward to his math classes. His teachers moved beyond commenting on his report cards that he was a diligent student to a 'prodigy' and 'whiz.' His love for numbers wasn't confined to his math textbook's neat rows and columns. It extended beyond the classroom, with a desire to learn about how math applied to the world of banking and finance.

One bright Spring day, as the end of his sophomore year approached, Ms. Thompson announced, "This assignment will be graded with your final term paper. So, please commit to working hard on it. You will likely think the topic is boring, but if you allow some creativity, it can be intriguing. I want your thorough research to be well-documented and referenced."

"How can she call this creative?" most students thought as they glanced at the handout. However, Graydon felt a peculiar spur within him. "I think this could be quite interesting."

He delved into the intricacies of the project with enthusiasm. He dove into the assigned readings, his brow furrowed in concentration as he unraveled the layers of the financial system. Once foreign to him, mortgage bonds, interest rates, and prepayment risk all these terms started to click into place. He spent his free time researching in the school library, watching topical videos, and even venturing into the local library to devour books on financial markets.

What seemed daunting to others became a fascinating puzzle for Graydon. He saw the elegance in the interconnectedness of interest rates, inflation, and housing prices. He marveled at how seemingly abstract concepts could have a tangible impact on people's lives. He calculated the economic impacts of different interest rate scenarios and sought to understand their intricacies. Being a number cruncher, this intensified his passion for finance.

Ms. Thompson was a seasoned educator with a keen eye for potential and recognized the unusual spark in Graydon. She saw beyond his diligence and good grades, spotting the genuine curiosity and thoughtfulness that went beyond rote learning.

One afternoon, after class, Ms. Thompson found Graydon analyzing a financial newspaper in the corner of the classroom. With a gentle smile, she approached him, "You seem quite engrossed in that section, Graydon. Anything in particular catching your eye?"

Graydon looked up, a mix of excitement and apprehension in his eyes. He explained his fascination with the intricate dance of numbers and their impact on the real world. Ms. Thompson listened intently, her smile widening as he spoke with a passion rarely seen for such complex topics. "You have a natural talent for understanding these systems, Graydon," she remarked, "and a hunger for knowledge that's truly commendable. Perhaps you should consider exploring finance further in your studies."

Those words, spoken with encouragement and genuine faith in his potential, served as a turning point for Graydon. The seed of interest, planted by a simple high school project, had blossomed into a genuine fascination with finance. It was the beginning of a journey that would lead him down a path where his aptitude and passion for numbers would intersect, shaping his future and paving the way for his eventual success.

Chapter 4: Youth

"Hey, Graydon. We've got a group heading over to Metro Grill. Would you care to join us?" asked one of his dormmates as they passed in the hallway.

"No, I'm good for now. I'm finishing some econ prep. But I may join you all later." Graydon replied with a polite smile, his mind still racing with assumptions and theories.

After Graydon graduated from high school, his passion for economics and finance took on a new intensity. While his dormmates and other friends would head out for the social scene and random festivities, Graydon found his true joy in number crunching and delving into the intricacies of financial markets. Most nights, he was tucked away in his room, pouring over textbooks on mortgage-backed securities and investment strategies. He easily grasped the algorithms and formulas, seeing patterns and potential where others saw only complexity.

While his friends joked about their future careers, Graydon was laser-focused. He made plans to make a significant impact in the finance world, revolutionizing how mortgage securities were analyzed and evaluated. His devotion was staunch, his purpose solid. Graydon understood that going into college, his path would not be the same as that of the others around him. It was not as if he did not enjoy the social scene; he did, occasionally venturing out with his friends, which usually ended at a nearby 24-hour café where they would spend hours discussing plans for their futures. He quickly became known as the "responsible one" who ensured that everyone made it back to their rooms safely.

The time he spent in college was driven by energy and tenacity. Early on, after being a part of study sessions, dorm room get-togethers, and various extracurricular activities, he was made aware of the Banking and Finance Studies group.

The BFS group was a haven for students like Graydon, who were passionate about finance, economics, and the intricate workings of the global markets. Led by a dedicated group of professors and industry professionals, the group provided a platform for students to engage in lively debates, organize guest lectures, and participate in hands-on workshops.

For Graydon, these gatherings were the highlight of his week. He was surrounded by like-minded individuals who shared his zeal for numbers and analysis. He felt a sense of belonging that he hadn't experienced before. The discussions ranged from the latest trends in the stock market to the implications of monetary policy on inflation rates, and he eagerly soaked up every bit of knowledge.

But it wasn't just about theoretical discussions for Graydon. The group also offered practical opportunities to apply their newfound knowledge in real-world scenarios. They organized stock trading competitions, where students could test their investment strategies and compete for prizes. He thrived in these challenges, meticulously researching companies, analyzing financial statements, and fine-tuning his portfolio to maximize returns.

In addition to the BFS group, Graydon also found himself drawn to the allure of the "Insomniacs," a rag-tag collection of socially awkward students who would convene in the library late at night till early in the morning. They celebrated caffeine in various forms as a vehicle to drive their discussions with purpose and determination to learn. Together, they conquered assignments, prepared for exams, thought 'outside the box,' and made the most of what others could bring to their various academic pursuits.

As Graydon navigated his college years, the BFS group remained a constant source of inspiration and motivation. It fueled his ambition, broadened his horizons, and solidified his passion for finance. Little did he know these formative experiences would lay the foundation for his future success in the world of ETFs and securities.

Before he set foot on campus, he had decided he wanted to make a difference in the world of finance. A simple observation during his first semester of Intro to Economics class confirmed his destiny.

Sitting in a crowded lecture hall, Graydon listened intently as the professor discussed mortgage-backed securities and their role in a financial crisis. When the lecturer proceeded to explore the finer details of the market, Graydon's analytical mind began to churn. He couldn't shake the feeling that there were faults in the way these securities were analyzed and evaluated. The formulas seemed outdated; the risk assessments were flawed. Graydon saw an opportunity to revolutionize the field, to create a system that could accurately predict and mitigate risks.

Wrought by this revelation, he threw himself into his studies with renewed vigor. He spent countless hours in the library, between classes, and with the Insomniacs, pouring over textbooks and academic journals. Driven to uncover the secrets of mortgage securities analytics, he sought out professors and experts in the field, peppering them with questions and soaking up their knowledge like a sponge.

His ambitions were not solely selfish. He saw the potential to not only advance his career but also to help others. He dreamed of creating a system to prevent another monetary crisis that would protect investors and homeowners alike. As he progressed through his college years, his passion only grew stronger. He refused to be deterred by setbacks or obstacles, viewing them as mere challenges to be overcome. And with each new hurdle conquered, his confidence soared.

One day, as he sat in the hushed atmosphere of the college library, surrounded by the scent of old books and the soft murmur of students immersed in their studies, he found himself engrossed in a particularly dense tome on financial analytics. Towering shelves of books and the soft rustle of pages turning, he delved into his latest research on mortgage-backed securities. The afternoon sunlight filtered through the dusty windows, casting long shadows across the rows of shelves, but he paid little heed to the passage of time. His attention was wholly consumed by the intricate world of mortgage-backed securities.

With furrowed brows and a pencil poised in hand, he pored over the text. His eyes scanned the pages with a keen intensity. Each sentence seemed to unlock new insights, each equation a puzzle waiting to be solved. As he flipped through the pages of an academic journal, his eyes caught on to a particular passage discussing the valuation models used for mortgage securities. Somewhere in the tangle of figures and formulas, something caught his attention. A subtle yet significant discrepancy lurked within the valuation models' framework. Frowning slightly, he paused, his analytical mind suspecting a potential flaw in the methodology.

The error lay in the assumptions underlying the valuation models. The models seemed to overlook certain key variables that could significantly impact the risk assessment of these securities. Graydon's pulse quickened as he realized the implications of his discovery. If these faults went unchecked, it could lead to inaccurate risk assessments and potentially catastrophic consequences for investors.

Excitement surged through him as he studied the models' subtleties more thoroughly, tracing the flaw back to its roots. It was a small oversight, perhaps unnoticed by many, but to Graydon, it represented a fundamental mistake in the way mortgage securities were being studied and assessed.

Intrigued to explore the matter deeper, Graydon spent the next few days immersing himself in research, cross-referencing diverse sources, and running simulations to test his hypothesis. With each passing hour, his conviction grew stronger. He had stumbled upon a critical drawback in the current approach to mortgage securities analytics, and he was resolute to address it.

Graydon spent the next few days immersed in research, combing through academic journals and consulting with experts in the field. With each new piece of evidence he uncovered, his hypothesis became much more theoretical and practical.

With his findings in hand, Graydon sought out one of his professors, Dr. Bauman, a renowned authority in financial modeling.

With a mixture of anticipation and apprehension swirling in his stomach, Graydon knocked lightly on the door of Dr. Bauman's office. The door swung open, revealing the cluttered yet inviting space within. Dr. Bauman looked up from his desk, his eyes crinkling in a warm smile as he gestured for Graydon to enter.

"Ah, Graydon, come in, come in," Dr. Bauman said, motioning toward a chair opposite his desk. "What brings you here today?"

Graydon took a deep breath, steeling himself for the conversation ahead. "Thank you, Dr. Bauman. I was hoping to speak with you about something I've been working on," he began, his voice steady despite the flutter of nerves in his chest.

"Of course. Please, have a seat," Dr. Bauman replied, leaning back in his chair with an encouraging nod. "What's on your mind?"

Graydon settled into the chair, his hands clasped tightly in his lap as he launched into an explanation of his research. "Well, sir, I've been delving into the valuation models used for mortgage-backed securities, and I've noticed a potential flaw in the assumptions underlying these models," he began, his words tumbling out in a rush of excitement and trepidation. The conversation took him back to his school days when he talked to his teacher about the school assignment he had done years ago in his economics class.

As he presented his research and outlined his concerns, he couldn't help but feel uncertainty. Would Dr. Bauman dismiss his findings as the ramblings of an overzealous student, or would he recognize the significance of what he had discovered?

Dr. Bauman listened intently, his brow furrowing in concentration as Graydon laid out his findings. With each point he made, he could see the interest in Dr. Bauman's eyes. He continued, "The current models fail to account for certain key variables that could significantly impact the risk assessment of these securities. By incorporating these variables into the models, we could provide a more accurate picture of the risks involved and potentially prevent future crises in the financial markets."

Dr. Bauman nodded thoughtfully, absorbing Graydon's explanation. "And you believe that by addressing this defect, we could improve the stability and resilience of the financial system?"

"Exactly," Graydon affirmed with a spark of excitement igniting in his eyes. "It's all about identifying and mitigating risks before they escalate into full-blown crises. With a more accurate assessment of risk, investors can make better-informed decisions, and regulators can take proactive measures to safeguard the stability of the financial markets."

Dr. Bauman leaned back in his chair, a thoughtful expression on his face. "I must say, Graydon, your findings are quite intriguing. This could indeed have far-reaching implications for the financial industry." To Graydon's relief and delight, Dr.

Bauman nodded in agreement, acknowledging the validity of his findings.

"Graydon, what you've uncovered here is truly remarkable," Dr. Bauman continued, his voice packed with admiration. "This flaw in the valuation models has far-reaching implications for the financial industry. If addressed, it could revolutionize the way we assess risk and make investment decisions."

A surge of pride and excitement welled up within Graydon as he absorbed Dr. Bauman's words. To have his work recognized and validated by such a respected authority was beyond his wildest dreams. With Dr. Bauman's encouragement ringing in his ears, Graydon threw himself into his research with revived intensity. He collaborated with fellow students and sought out feedback from industry professionals, refining his methodologies and developing innovative solutions to address the issue.

Months passed, and Graydon's research gained momentum within academic circles. He presented his findings at conferences, published papers in prestigious journals, and even caught the attention of a few industry leaders who were novices in the market for now. They all were eager to learn more about his groundbreaking work.

And then, one fateful day, as Graydon sat focusing on a particularly dense research paper on exchange-traded funds (ETFs), inspiration struck like a bolt of lightning. It was a moment of clarity and a sudden realization that would change the course of his life forever.

At that moment, Graydon had found a piece of information about ETF rebalancing that completed a formula in his economic forecasting model. With this formula, he thought one could revolutionize the manner in which investors accessed and diversified their portfolios, offering unparalleled flexibility, transparency, and efficiency. It was a bold concept that pushed the boundaries of conventional thinking and promised to disrupt the financial industry's status quo.

When he graduated, Graydon was already well on his way to achieving his dreams. Armed with a wealth of knowledge and a fierce strength of mind, he set out into the financial world, ready to make his mark.

As he stood on the precipice of greatness in the New York Stock Exchange, poised to ring the bell after launching his groundbreaking ETF onto the world stage, Graydon felt a sense of gratitude for the transformative power of his college experience. For it was there, amidst the hustle and bustle of campus life, that his passion had been ignited, his ambition had been polished, and his dreams had taken flight.

However, the true measure of success he knew would not come from accolades or recognition but from the knowledge that he would make a tangible impact on the world around him. With each step forward, he moved closer to his ultimate goal. And as he looked toward the future, he knew that the pace of his journey was shifting into a higher gear.

Chapter 5: Early Triumphs

Graydon had poured his heart and soul into his college project on the faults in valuation models used for mortgage-backed securities. His presentation on the project was met with a mix of intrigue and skepticism from his peers and professors. Some questioned his findings, while others were impressed by the thoroughness of his analysis. He was invited to present at an International Financial Conference.

Although Graydon hoped, he did not expect his presentation to change the course of his life. Amongst the audience were several representatives from numerous Wall Street firms who were intrigued by the boldness and intelligence displayed in his work. A half dozen or so were quick to raise their hands during the Q&A that followed, with each of them satisfied with Graydon's answers and further comments. One knew immediately that Graydon had a keen analytical mind and a unique ability to think freely, an asset his firm needed.

Shortly after the Q&A ended, he approached Graydon, who recognized him as an author of several financial newsletters he had reviewed earlier in the year. He was from what Graydon considered to be the top investment bank on Wall Street. Within a few minutes of their conversation, he offered him a paid internship, stating he was impressed by his project, his passion for finance, and his drive to challenge conventional methods. This was the opportunity Graydon had dreamt of, and he could hardly believe it was really happening. As he accepted, he knew his life at this point was set on the best trajectory he could hope for.

Graydon's internship was a journey marked by sincerity and innovation. He faced many difficulties and struggles but always adapted and completed his work. Armed with his keen intellect and limitless curiosity, he dove headfirst into the world of Wall Street, eager to carve a path for his future. As his internship progressed, Graydon found himself further drawn to the intersection of finance and technology. He saw the immense possibility of success and profit in employing the power of supercomputing via quantitative analysis and machine learning. He felt it could revolutionize monetary modeling and trading strategies. He began experimenting with early versions of AI algorithms, exceeding the boundaries of the standards of the times.

At first, his colleagues were skeptical and wary of venturing into unfamiliar territory. But Graydon's passion and conviction were infectious, and soon, he had a small team of like-minded individuals improving his vision. Together, they worked tirelessly and tried to fine-tune algorithms and test hypotheses. They were on an insistent quest for reliability and, thus, profitability.

Soon, by using early versions of quant analysis-driven models, Graydon discovered hidden patterns and correlations in market data, identifying lucrative opportunities that had previously gone unnoticed. Whether it was predicting shifts in commodity prices or identifying undervalued assets in emerging markets, his model consistently outperformed traditional methods, delivering impressive returns for the firm. Word of his success spread quickly throughout Wall Street, earning him a reputation in the world of quantitative finance.

Graydon remained humble, always quick to credit his team and acknowledge the contributions of those who had supported him along the way. Despite his success, Graydon never lost sight of the ethical implications of his work. He was acutely aware of the dangers of unchecked algorithmic trading, recognizing the responsibility that came with this powerful influence. He advocated for greater transparency and accountability in the use of supercomputing in fiscal matters. Pushing for industry-wide standards, he ensured that the benefits of technological innovation were shared equitably among all stakeholders.

As he looked back on his journey, Graydon couldn't help but marvel at how far he had come from a college project that challenged the assumptions underlying traditional valuation models to a pioneering force at the forefront of quant-driven finance.

Upon graduation, Graydon was inundated with offers from all the top-tier financial institutions eager to benefit from his talent and expertise. However, one stood far above the rest. It included a generous signing bonus, competitive salary, and profit-sharing incentives with a promise to establish his own investment office funded with a ten million dollar budget, the highest amount the firm had ever provided to a recent college grad hire. This was an opportunity that Graydon was hoping for. With the backing of such substantial capital, he thought he was assured of having the resources to pursue his goal.

Graydon charted a bold course for his investment office, drawing on the experience and insights he gained from his college project and internship. Rather than focusing solely on traditional asset classes, he sought to diversify the fund's holdings across a wide range of markets and strategies.

With his background in supercomputing, Graydon saw an opportunity to leverage technology. To gain a competitive edge in the economic trading world, he invested heavily in innovative quant codes that were designed to analyze vast amounts of data. They also identified hidden patterns and opportunities in the market. The results were nothing short of spectacular. In only a few years, Graydon's investment office became one of the most profitable divisions within the firm as they delivered consistently high returns across all asset classes. His uncanny ability to check out volatile markets and capitalize on emerging trends earned him a reputation as a visionary investor and a trusted steward of capital.

As the fund continued to grow, Graydon remained committed and reinvested profits back into the business, expanding the team and further bringing high-tech resources. He also sought out new opportunities to give back to the community, supporting charitable initiatives. He helped with educational programs that were aimed at encouraging the next generation of commercial trade. Regardless of his hectic schedule and the demands of running the investment operation, Graydon always made time for his friends and his family. He cherished moments spent with loved ones, finding much-needed normalcy in them.

Every Sunday evening, without fail, he would call home to check in and see how his folks were doing. Every time, his mother would answer. Their conversations were deep and meaningful. He knew by the second ring he would hear her voice at the other end of the line.

"Hi, Mom," Graydon would say with affection.

"Graydon, darling! How lovely to hear your voice," his mother would reply with joy at the sound of her son's voice.

They would catch up on the day's events, the latest news from home, updates on his father and sister, and stories from Graydon's work life. His mother would listen intently as Graydon would recount his challenges and successes, offering words of encouragement and wisdom whenever he needed them. No matter how busy Graydon's schedule became, he always made sure to ask the same question before ending the call, "Are you okay, Mom?"

And every time he asked, his mother's response was the same, "Yes, Graydon, I'm okay. Don't worry about me. Just take care of yourself and keep doing what you're doing. And don't forget to take your vitamins!"

***

One evening, as Graydon was winding down at his apartment after a long day at the office, his phone buzzed. It was a message from his parents' friends, the Bay's. As Graydon sat down to read the message, memories of the time he spent at their house as a young teenager flooded his mind. It had been years since he had last seen them. He could almost hear Mrs. Bay's quirky laughter and Mr. Bay's hearty jokes. It had been far too long, so he felt a bit guilty about not staying in touch more regularly.

"Hi, Graydon. This is Mr. Bay." The message read.

Graydon typed out his response, *"Hi, Mr. Bay! It's been too long, hasn't it? I hope you and Mrs. Bay are doing well."*

The reply came swiftly, *"Graydon, it's wonderful to reach you! We've missed you too. I'll call you now."* And just like that, Graydon's phone rang. Wondering why this sudden need to connect, he answered.

"Hey, Mr. Bay," he said.

"Hey Graydon, how are you, my boy?" A cheery sound came at the other end of the line.

"I'm doing well, thank you. Now you tell me. How are you?"

Mr. Bay replied, his tone just as friendly. "I've been well too, thank you."

"Great," Graydon replied while looking at a stack of documents on his coffee table. "How's everything with you and Mrs. Bay?"

"Oh, you know, the usual," Mr. Bay said with a chuckle. "Mrs. Bay has been keeping herself occupied with her gardening. She's still as passionate about it as ever."

Graydon couldn't help but smile at her obsession with gardening. "Some things never change, huh? How's her prized rose bush doing?"

"It's flourishing, as always," Mr. Bay replied fondly. "She's been spending hours tending to it every week."

"That's wonderful to hear," Graydon said. "And how's the weather been over your way?"

Mr. Bay sighed lightly. "Oh, you know how it is this time of year. One day, it's sunny; the next, it's pouring rain. Can't seem to make up its mind."

Graydon nodded in understanding. "Same here. We've had quite a mix of weather lately. Makes planning outdoor activities a bit tricky."

"Indeed," Mr. Bay agreed. "Speaking of which, have you had any chance to get out and enjoy the outdoors yourself?"

Graydon shook his head regretfully. "Not as much as I'd like, unfortunately. Work has been keeping me tied up lately, but you know, I really enjoy it. I did manage to go for a hike last weekend with some college friends that were in town, which was nice."

"Ah, good for you!" Mr. Bay exclaimed. "Life has been keeping us busy as well, but we're always grateful for the chance to reconnect with old friends. And speaking of work, your dad has told us about your job and achievements. Congratulations, Graydon! We couldn't be prouder of you." Graydon couldn't help but smile at the kind words.

"Thank you so much, Mr. Bay," Graydon replied. "How about you? What are you up to these days? Have you been able to find some time for leisure activities?"

Mr. Bay chuckled again. "Oh, you know me. Between the lawn and various household projects, it feels like there's always something to be done. But I did manage to sneak in a round of golf last week with two of my old co-workers."

"A good walk spoiled, eh?" Graydon said with a grin. "One of the last times I played was with you all."

"Set some time aside next time you're here and we will attack the course again. It would be great to catch up in person while playing golf."

"Definitely," Graydon agreed. "I hope it will happen soon."

"But for now, I'm calling to ask if you would consider meeting someone who's about to move near you."

"Who would that be?" Graydon began speculating about who it could be and why Mr. Bay would want him to meet them.

"Do you remember my niece, Sophie?" Mr. Bay questioned.

"Sophie... hmm," Graydon gave it thought. "I can't place her."

"Well, you were young when she visited us, and the next time she came, you were off to college. Anyway, your parents and I had dinner together last weekend, and Sophie came up in our conversation because she's moving to your area. Mrs. Bay and I are thinking that you two should connect." Mr. Bay's voice seemed to race faster.

"Connect?" Graydon instantly knew where this was going and now found their conversation a bit awkward.

"You know, just get to know each other. She doesn't know anyone there. I thought it'd be best for her to meet someone nice right off the bat. Lord knows I don't think there are many nice young men left. We're planning on helping her with her move and thought perhaps we could all have dinner together?" Mr. Bay now sounded hopeful.

"Well, first off, what day and time?" Graydon said with hesitance.

"Next Thursday, the 11th, at 7 P.M. You choose the place." Mr. Bay suggested.

"Okay, text me the details on where you'll be staying, and I'll pick a spot nearby that's worthy of your presence. Now, sometimes my schedule gets bumped around, so I'll plan to confirm with you the day before."

"Sounds perfect. See you soon!" with that, their call ended.

The conversation with Mr. Bay had Graydon's mind racing. A combination of confusion, embarrassment, and nervousness was clouding his thoughts. Mr. Bay's request to re-introduce him to his niece, Sophie, left Graydon perplexed and unsure how to react. Sophie was essentially a stranger to him, and the thought of meeting her under such circumstances made him uneasy. What was he supposed to say? What if they had nothing in common? The mere idea of the encounter filled him with a sense of awkwardness. He was no stranger to social interactions, but this felt different.

With a sigh and shrug of his shoulders, Graydon realized that he couldn't avoid it. *'Just leave it to good fate from family friends,'* he thought as he headed to bed.

Chapter 6: Meeting the Love

Graydon sat at one corner of the long table, intently focusing on his plate as if it held the secrets of the universe, hoping to divert attention from him. Nervousness prickled at his skin, making him aware of every sound, every movement around him. Despite his best efforts to appear engaged, his mind was elsewhere, trying to make sense of this dinner he tried to avoid.

On Wednesday, he texted Mr. Bay that his schedule had changed and Thursday evening would not work. A few hours later, his parents called to say they decided to come in for the weekend with their friends, the Wellings, and everyone should meet for dinner on Saturday. Graydon made reservations for 7:00 p.m. at a quaint Italian restaurant that he admired not just because of their atmosphere and food but also because of their ornate copper-clad cappuccino maker.

The Wellings family was a picture-perfect family with elegance and refinement. Their presence created a graceful yet cherished aura over the dinner table. Mr. Wellings, with his silver hair and distinguished demeanor, held court at one end of the table. Regaling the guests with tales of his travels and adventures, he was the life of the party. His wife exuded warmth and hospitality. Her gentle smile and welcoming manners put everyone at ease. Their daughter, Martha, was a youthful, energetic, and vivacious girl. Her laughter was vividly audible as she engaged in animated conversation with the other guests. Her enthusiasm lit up the room, drawing people toward her with effortless charm.

On the other side of the table sat Thomas, the Wellings' son. He was a quiet and introspective young man who observed the proceedings with a thoughtful look. Despite his youthful age, he possessed a reserved nature. There was a depth to him that indicated the possibility of a rich inner life. And of course, there between his mother and Mrs. Bay sat Sophie.

The restaurant exuded an avant-garde posh ambiance and was always filled with more from nearby than tourists. Graydon had selected this location not just because it was convenient for everyone but because the tantalizing aroma of garlic, basil, and simmering marinara sauce wafting from the open kitchen always reminded him of his favorite meal from home. Soft, golden light spilled from wrought-iron sconces lining the walls and formed intricate patterns of shadows across the rustic, terracotta-colored tiles underfoot. All the tables were arranged in neat rows draped in crisp, starched white linens and adorned with vintage Chianti bottles topped with slow-burning candles that added a romantic glow to the room. Masterful paintings of pastoral landscapes were hanging on the walls, transporting diners to the sun-drenched hills of Tuscany with their vibrant colors and serene beauty. The soft sound of Italian music flowed from hidden speakers as the wait staff glided effortlessly between tables, all uniformly dressed in white dress shirts with black vests, trousers, and shoes.

At the center of the restaurant stood the bustling open kitchen. Its stainless-steel surfaces gleamed under the spotlights as chefs worked their craft, showcasing a variety of hand-crafted pasta and sauces with skill and precision. The aroma of freshly baked bread, garlic, olive oil, and simmering sauces was tantalizing.

The clinking of cutlery against plates was indistinctive from the table's ongoing conversations. Mr. Bay's hearty laugh would echo across the table from time to time, while Mrs. Bay's dulcet tones would balance and soften the volume.

But for Graydon, any noise only served to amplify his sense of unease. He was quietly observant and joined when asked questions directly. He kept his answers brief as his thoughts were fixated on Sophie, this striking young woman with a soft glow around her, like a halo, whom he was supposed to meet.

He noticed she sat with an air of quiet confidence; her posture was relaxed yet poised. A subtle grace was evident in her every movement. Her deep blue eyes sparkled in a manner that conveyed her self-assurance, which was rooted deeply within. She had an engaging manner and style that were so alluring it was difficult for him to take his eyes off her.

As her eyes wandered to the other side of the room, her gaze met Graydon's. She smiled meekly as she shifted her eyes back to the others. And then back to him. This time, it was not the same.

For a brief moment, time seemed to stand still. A silent connection formed between them as if their lives were pointing toward this moment. In that fleeting instant, Graydon felt something unfamiliar stir within him with a gentle insistence that he could not comprehend. Suddenly, he became self-conscious of their locked eyes. He knew something extraordinary was happening.

Meanwhile, Mr. and Mrs. Wellings had been describing their recent family trip to France and all the patisseries they'd visited. Oblivious to the silent exchange between Graydon and Sophie, Mr. Wellings asked Graydon directly, "Have you thought about taking a few months off to travel?" *'Ugh!'* thought Graydon as he had to try to formulate an answer. "I hope to do so sometime soon" was the best he could think of. "What about you Sophie?" Mrs. Wellings asked.

As she began to answer, Graydon wondered, *'What is this? This was arranged for Sophie and me to get to know each other. Why is this the first moment they draw us in when I seemingly connect with her?'* "I've always dreamed of going for an extended time with the right person," she said with a wry smile. *'Well, there's the answer!'* Graydon thought. *'If she gets up and heads to the ladies' room, I'm getting up too.'*

But as the minutes ticked by, Sophie remained firmly seated, caught in another conversation with Mrs. Bay, Mrs. Wellings, and Martha. Graydon's frustration mounted with each passing second. His impatience was reaching its end beneath the surface. He glanced at his watch, wishing time would move faster, but it just dragged on at a snail's pace.

And so, Graydon remained in his seat, silently willing Sophie to excuse herself. He watched her intently, his heart pounding in his chest as he waited for the moment when she would finally rise from her chair and give him an opportunity to approach her. Even a slight creak that her chair made riveted his attention, hoping that it signaled she was getting up.

Eventually, as the dessert plates were cleared away, Graydon's thoughts shifted. The moment for a private conversation with Sophie had slipped away as the bill arrived. At last, with resignation, Graydon leaned in close to his mother, his voice barely above a whisper. "I'm going over to the bar for a moment to order Alfredo to go for tomorrow's lunch. I'll be right back."

His mother nodded understandingly, a knowing smile playing at the corners of her lips. With a grateful smile, Graydon slipped away from the table. His footsteps echoed softly against the tiled floor as he made his way to the bar. The handmade Alfredo was his favorite, always reminding him of home, which he often longed for, particularly in moments of uncertainty.

As Graydon headed toward the bar, a familiar face greeted him with a warm smile and a friendly nod. It was Tony who had served him numerous times before.

"Alfredo to go, right?" Tony said with a knowing grin and a bit of amusement.

Graydon chuckled, nodding in affirmation. "You know me too well, Tony," he replied with a smile. "Can't resist it."

Tony chuckled in response, heading over to the kitchen without needing to ask for further details. As was the case with other customers, he knew Graydon's order and the days and times he was likely to stop by.

A few minutes passed before Tony reappeared, handing over a to-go bag. The alluring aroma elicited a contented sigh from Graydon as he settled back against the bar, allowing himself a moment of quiet reflection. In the middle of the bustling restaurant, surrounded by all the sights and sounds, his thoughts drifted back to the dinner table and Sophie.

Graydon couldn't stop himself from thinking about the look they exchanged. Lost in contemplation, he barely noticed when Tony's voice broke through his reverie.

"Fun night?" Tony inquired as he tilted his head toward their table. "It would be if it was a party of two," Graydon said with a hopeful tone.

Tony nodded understandingly, his expression one of genuine care. "Can I help?" he asked. Instantly, a light bulb flashed in Graydon's mind. "Yes, actually," Graydon replied, "I'm going to stand here and write a note for the young woman at the far end of our table."

Tony looked up and caught on to the woman Graydon spoke of, "Oh, yeah. I see. The one wearing the yellow sweater, right? Looks like she's got a halo over those beautiful golden curls, eh?" he remarked.

"Right!" Graydon affirmed. "I'm going to write a note. Would you take this over to her when I leave? I'll come back in an hour or so."

With a sense of purpose, Graydon quickly scribbled a message on the note. His hand trembling slightly with nervous anticipation. He addressed it to Sophie,

"I enjoyed meeting you this evening and would like to visit again soon. I'll be back here in an hour. Is there any chance you can stop by, too? If not, perhaps next week? :-)"

-Graydon

As he folded the note and handed it to Tony, Graydon felt a surge of hopeful excitement. Tony took the note and pen that Graydon had procured from the bar counter, and with a wink and a smile, he said, "No problem. Consider it done."

"I'll see you in an hour," Graydon said over his shoulder as he headed back to the table. A few minutes later, the dinner party began to disperse, bidding their farewells with promises to meet again soon. As Graydon stood up, he noticed a twinge of disappointment in Sophie's expression. He fought to contain a grin forming from his thought of what her expression would be when Tony handed her his note.

As he walked down the block, he looked up between the high rises at the night sky and thought and was certain he caught a glimpse of a shooting star falling from the heavens. *'Ah, that's divine,'* he thought to himself.

Chapter 7: Passions

As Graydon walked around the enormous conference table, his eyes swept over the ostentatiously appointed chairs. Pausing at the far end to gaze out at the impressive city view from the top floor, he stood tall.

"How often do you fill this room?" he inquired, his voice carrying a note of curiosity.

The eldest attorney, a distinguished figure with silver hair and a somber expression, paused momentarily before responding. "I would say twice a month," he replied slowly, in a measured and authoritative tone.

Mr. and Mrs. Maxwell, accompanied by their attorney, had arrived to sign the documents. It was the closing day for their purchase of the investment company. Excited as they were, they entered the room with a cherished glow yet a composed countenance. However, they hadn't anticipated being greeted by the sight of seven other attorneys and five bankers gathered in the room. The seating for thirty suddenly felt cramped and crowded.

Graydon glanced around the table and saw Sophie's mind at work. Her wheels turned as she silently surveyed the scene. He knew she was calculating every detail, meticulously assessing what this legal bill would mean for their finances. Although they were about to sign a 10 Million Dollar loan, every cent mattered to her.

After what felt like an eternity of shuffling papers to review and sign, the tension in the room began to dissipate. As the fourteenth signature page was completed, one of the attorneys rose from his seat and crossed over to the antique sideboard. He picked up the phone, dialed a number, and spoke in a commanding tone. "Send the wires," he instructed.

At that moment, a sense of relief and accomplishment washed over him. As the sound of the dial tone echoed through the room, Graydon couldn't help but feel a swell of pride. With the paperwork complete, Graydon turned to Sophie, a silent understanding passing between them. They had steered through the complexities of the legal process together. Now, when they were emerging victorious in their pursuit of financial success, Graydon only looked at Sophie, his memory fixed on their first meeting at dinner when she'd first moved to the city.

***

Graydon sat perched on a stool at the counter with a cappuccino in his hand. His gaze remained fixed on the entrance. Nearby was Tony, who always conversed with customers and staff in an air of warm hospitality.

"So, you think she will appear?" Graydon asked with anticipation and uncertainty as Tony passed by.

Tony flashed him a reassuring smile. "Without a doubt," he replied. "I saw the look on her face. Trust me, she's going to be here any minute now."

Graydon nodded, sipping his drink as he mulled over Tony's words. He couldn't help but feel a surge of nerves coursing through him. His heart visibly pounded as he anticipated Sophie's arrival.

"Did she say anything when you handed her the note?" Graydon pressed, his curiosity getting the better of him.

Tony shook his head. "She just thanked me," he replied. "Oh, and her face lit up when she smiled."

As if on cue, the door swung open, and Sophie stepped into the restaurant, her presence commanding attention as she crossed the threshold. The atmosphere seemed to shift in her wake. The energy in the room palpably changed as her eyes scanned the room. Graydon's breath caught in his throat as he looked at her. His heart skipped a beat at the sight of her. She was a vision of beauty and grace. Her eyes glinted with a glowing intensity. He was like a moth, attracted to the flame, or in his case, her glory. However, she was not a fire that would burn him but one that would ignite his ambitions into action and provide him with the warmth he needed.

As Sophie made her way toward him, her smile radiated in such a manner that Graydon was instantly captivated by her presence. He could not take his eyes off her. As she drew closer, his pulse noticeably quickened. When she reached his side, her warm greeting ignited a wonderful sense of excitement and joy.

"Hi, Graydon," she spoke in a soft tone, extending her hand for a shake. Graydon was transfixed, standing with silent admiration. She raised a curious eyebrow.

"Graydon," Tony blurted, causing him to blink, snapping out of his daze as he turned to Tony and back to her with a sheepish grin. "Oh, hey," he managed, finally reaching out to shake her hand. "Thanks for coming back. Please, have a seat. Care for a cappuccino? Their la Pavoni espresso machine was custom-made and imported from Italy."

Sophie nodded in acknowledgment, taking the seat next to him. For a moment, there was an awkward silence as they both struggled to find something to say. Finally, Graydon broke the ice.

"Um, it was weird how we got introduced," he began tentatively, prompting a nod of agreement from Sophie. "I mean, in such a traditional way."

"I was a bit unsure about it," she admitted with a slight smirk. Her eyes met his in understanding.

"So, what brought you to the city?" Graydon asked, eager to keep the conversation going.

Sophie nodded, her expression brightening. "Oh, I took a job here," she replied.

"Really? What kind of work?" he inquired eagerly.

"I work in finance," Sophie revealed in a modest tone. Graydon's eyes lit up with genuine interest. "You know, I'm working with a firm on Wall Street. We're using this new supercomputing technique to optimize our funds," he explained with excitement, which was evident in his voice.

"Oh, really?" Sophie's eyes sparkled with intrigue. "I've always been fascinated by the new concepts in the financial system."

The next hour seemed to fly by as they dug into a deeper discussion about their shared values and aspirations for success. Their connection grew stronger with each passing moment. In their shared enthusiasm for innovation and progress, they found a common bond that drew them together, setting the stage for an exhilarating ride ahead. It was that day and then today, when they were signing for the company, that they had crossed a long path with each other's support and collective interests.

***

As he thought about first meeting Sophie and the success they had achieved together, he could not help but reflect on his first banking job. During his junior year at Grove High, he met with one of the guidance counselors who asked, "Are you set on Circle College?" with a hint of concern. "I don't see any hurdles if you care to apply elsewhere."

Graydon turned toward him after scanning his office bookcases and noting the titles. "Yes, I'm set on Circle," he replied confidently. "They have plenty of subjects I'm interested in at different times, so I can schedule classes in a manner that appeals to me, and I'll still have room for part-time work if I get bored. But what I really hope happens is a chance to do research because I think that experience would add greater value to my resume and increase my opportunities."

His guidance counselor nodded with a thoughtful expression. "Just don't go overboard on work or research," he cautioned. "A few hours a week makes sense, but focus on finishing in four years. You've done well here. Keep it up!"

The work ethic instilled by his parents was a quality and characteristic that his neighbors had come to recognize in him as well. During high school, several neighbors asked him to do regular tasks like cutting lawns, raking leaves, and trimming bushes and shrubs.

The Hopkins, whose home was just down the street, was one of his first customers. Mr. Hopkins, a Vice President of Consumer Lending at First Citizens Bank, had taken notice of Graydon's thoroughness and work ethic. "You ought to apply for a part-time Teller position," he suggested shortly after Graydon's sixteenth birthday. "The hours are flexible; you'd be working inside and gaining some valuable experience. Let me know if you'd like an introduction to our personnel manager."

The campus norm for juniors and seniors at Grove High School was to be gone by 1 P.M. After visiting Mr. Hopkins further, Graydon consulted with his parents and decided to apply for the position. After three rounds of interviews, he was offered a part-time position as a drive-thru teller at First Citizens Bank.

Each day, after finishing his classes, Graydon would make his way to the bank, ready to tackle whatever tasks awaited him. From assisting customers with their transactions to balancing the cash drawers at the end of the day, he approached his work with professionalism.

Working indoors as a teller at First Citizens Bank was a welcome change for Graydon. While the main bank was nearby, the drive-thru branch remained bustling with activity throughout the day. Graydon enjoyed the interactions with the customers and his fellow staff members.

Friendly competition was a constant presence among the tellers. Each one of the workers strived to balance speed and accuracy to the penny. Graydon took pride in his ability to manage transactions while maintaining a keen eye for detail efficiently. He relished the challenge and friendship that came with working alongside his colleagues.

Various executive management staff would occasionally stop by the bank for a brief visit. They would offer their insights and thoughts on various banking and customer service subjects. Graydon welcomed these interactions as he was eager to learn from those with more experience and expertise in the field.

The distance from Grove High to the bank made it easy for Graydon to shift from his academic responsibilities to his work obligations. After a mere ten-minute walk, he would arrive at the bank ready to tackle the afternoon shift, which lasted until 6 P.M.

Despite the demanding nature of his schedule, Graydon saw each day as an opportunity to gain experience and learn, both professionally and personally. This flourished a sense of purpose and fulfillment from balancing school and work.

Seniors were allowed to craft their schedules if they had completed the standard requirements for graduation, which, of course, Graydon had. So, he locked in the remaining business and finance classes he had not taken and filled in the rest with elective courses unrelated to business. There were some interesting characters in his elective classes, bringing a unique eccentric energy and personality to the classroom.

While Graydon was certain that some of these characters would fade into the background after graduation, he couldn't deny their value to the learning experience. Their quirks and insights reminded him of his parent's belief to "Always look for the good in unexpected places."

Chapter 8: Marriage

Just before 5:30 A.M., as the light of a new day began to dawn, Graydon awakened from his sleep. With a sense of purpose, he rose from his bed and moved quickly to begin his morning routine. Time was marching on, and in the early morning sun, the promise of a fresh start prepared him to tackle the day ahead.

As he dropped into his office chair, Graydon noticed he was the only new hire to arrive before 7:00 A.M. The early morning hours were quiet, and only a handful of others moved about the floor. It wasn't until just before 8:00 a.m. that the rest of the staff came in suddenly like a herd of cattle.

Among the early handful was Vance, a fellow analyst who started a year ago with whom Graydon had built a friendly rapport. As they exchanged greetings, he commented on the early hour. "Seems like we're the only ones that are regularly here bright and early."

Graydon chuckled, "Guess we're the only ones that don't stay out all night and can function early in the morning."

As the day progressed, Graydon found himself absorbed in his work. He filtered through results with each report, carefully analyzing the data and noting any emerging trends or patterns.

The office was always active and busy as Graydon sat intently before his dual monitors amidst the clatter of keyboards and the occasional ring of phones.

He took notes constantly. He was told his brow would furrow occasionally while he analyzed data sets. He became unaware of everything in the office; everything around him turned into a blur, including the constant sounds around him, which his keyboard contributed to.

While paging through a report, he heard a cheerful voice. "How's it going, Graydon?" Mr. Jenkins, his supervisor, asked as he approached with a friendly smile.

Graydon looked up and replied. "Busy as usual, sir." He gestured toward the screens. "Just trying to make sense of the latest sales data from the new economic numbers."

Mr. Jenkins leaned in and glanced at the charts. Graydon clicked on a graph and enlarged it. "There are some promising trends. The initial response rates have exceeded our projections in several regions. It might be worth exploring why they're performing so well."

"That's what I like to hear," Mr. Jenkins placed a hand on Graydon's shoulder, a gesture of support. "Keep up the excellent work. It's this kind of initiative that drives our success. Let me know if you need anything from me."

"Will do, sir. Thanks," Graydon said, returning his gaze to the monitor as Mr. Jenkins moved away, mingling back into the flow of the office. Graydon continued his work.

***

Trojan Hedge Funds had made the offer that stood far above the rest. Mr. Jenkins had attended the International Financial Conference that Graydon presented at and reported to the Executive Management Committee that Graydon was the only upcoming graduate he wanted to pursue. He mentioned to them that in his conversation with Graydon, he had already studied THF's balance sheet, income statement, and articles on their strategies focused on mortgage-backed securities and, with that knowledge, offered his initial comments and observations, one of which Mr. Jenkins had already implemented.

One of Graydon's first tasks was to report on the difference between expected and actual cash flow for Trojan's "Primary Mortgage Fund." Addition and subtraction seemed to be all that was required for this task. Equipped with more than that, he set to work with ease. With the reports completed in record time, Graydon had more than enough time to ponder the discrepancies he had uncovered. It soon became apparent that more cash flow was being received monthly than expected. This was puzzling to him, and he thought it demanded further investigation.

Graydon's brow furrowed as he dug deeper into the numbers; his instincts told him something was off. As he pulled up the models, his heart rate quickened. What he found was shocking. He took another look at the numbers. The data was indeed flawed. He realized that the algorithm, which was supposed to be a sophisticated tool, was barely scraping the surface. It used just a few broad inputs to predict what was represented to be complex, mortgage-backed securities cash flows. "Speed," a critical factor, was updated monthly, but it was treated as a vague average rather than reflecting the unique characteristics of each security.

Graydon leaned closer to his screen and rapidly tapped the keyboard as he cross-checked the figures. The realization hit him like a cold splash of water: they were flying blind with faulty instruments. This wasn't just a minor oversight but a gaping hole in their financial modeling. He knew he couldn't sit on this. It was too big, too risky.

After confirming his suspicions about the faulty modeling, Graydon leaned back in his chair. He couldn't keep it to himself. He glanced at the clock on his computer—it was Friday, and trading hours had ended much earlier. He packed up his things and decided to walk the long route home. He had found a piece of significant information, and now he was ready to display his findings to his supervisors.

***

That Sunday evening, when Graydon called home, he was more than ready to share this news with his parents. "Hey, Mom, can you ask Dad to pick up the other phone?"

"Of course, how's everything?" his mother's voice came through as he heard his father moving in the background.

"Everything's fine. I do have something important to discuss. I've found a significant flaw in the financial models we use at work. It's about the 'Speed' input in our projections. It's all wrong, generalized far too much for something crucial."

There was a pause on the other end as his parents digested the news. Then his father responded. "Son, that sounds like a significant issue. But you need to be careful. How do you plan to proceed?"

Graydon sighed. "I want to bring this up to my superiors. I think it's important, but I wanted to get your take first."

"Graydon, we're proud you caught this, but remember, you're still new there. They might not take it well to hear such news coming from someone who hasn't been around long. Maybe keep it to yourself for a while?"

Graydon nodded to himself, considering his parents' advice. "I understand your concern. It's just hard to sit on something like this."

"We know, dear, but sometimes timing is as important as the information. Just be sure when you decide to share this, you're fully prepared for any consequences," his father advised wisely.

They suggested Graydon continue refining his model and gathering evidence to validate his work. They added that he could use his expertise to carve out his path within the company if successful.

After a lengthy discussion, they ended the call. Graydon knew his parents were right about the risks, yet the weight of his responsibility to his findings was heavy on his mind.

***

In the coming days, Graydon followed his parents' advice. He kept working on and used his methods to come up with a plan to generate more revenue. He continued to refine his model and, drawing inspiration from the results, began to explore the potential of purchasing ETFs as part of his fund management strategy.

ETFs offered him a unique opportunity to expand the fund's portfolio and provide investors with access to a broader range of assets. Graydon saw them as a way to democratize investing, allowing the general public to benefit in the same ways traditionally reserved for wealthy clients.

While all of this was going on in his life, Sophie's presence was calming for him, and as they discussed the nuances of the model, their understanding deepened. It was not the first time she had helped him or appreciated his efforts; this had become a ritual for her.

In the following weeks, Graydon and Sophie collaborated on more projects. Their teamwork was seamless, and their after-work conversations grew longer and deeper. They started spending all their free time together outside of work, exploring city parks, visiting local bookstores, and enjoying quiet dinners. Their connection was immediate and undeniable. It sparked a romance that swept them off their feet, and they both knew they were meant to be together.

Sophie even stood with him throughout his mission of refining the MBS model. She understood him, helped him, and encouraged him in what he believed. It was during these sessions that Graydon realized how much Sophie had become a pivotal part of his life. He had decided he would not let her go, and he would ask her to spend the rest of her life with him.

***

One evening, Graydon and Sophie were sitting on their favorite park bench. It was a spot that had become special to them as they had spent countless evenings sitting and talking on it. As they watched the sunset, Sophie leaned her head on Graydon's shoulder and could hear the soft, comforting rhythm of his heartbeat. They watched in silence, appreciating the beauty of the sunset and the quiet comfort of each other's presence.

Just then, Graydon turned to Sophie and took her hand in his, feeling the softness of her touch.

"What?" she whispered while shifting her head.

"Sophie," Graydon looked into her eyes and found the future he wanted forever to hold. "These past months with you have been the happiest of my life. Every moment we've shared has only made me more certain that I want to spend all my days with you."

Sophie's eyes glistened with emotion as she squeezed his hand, encouraging him to continue.

"I know it's us... forever," Graydon watched her face as he spoke. He hoped to see the same feelings in her that he felt deep within him.

Sophie smiled. "Forever," she said softly, resting her head on his shoulder again.

They remained on the bench, holding hands, lost in each other's presence. They didn't need a grand proposal or dramatic declarations; their commitment was forged in the everyday moments of companionship and mutual support.

Like their love, their engagement was genuine and simple yet profoundly deep. They were blown over from day one, not by their spontaneous love or connection, but by the understanding and support they had worked on together. They were meant to be; they had known that first day, and every day after that confirmed it.

"Let's get married as soon as possible!" they both said. That was all they needed. Full of excitement and anticipation, they rushed back to the quaint Italian restaurant where they had first met. Tony's familiar face greeted them with a warm smile as they made their way past the tables to the bar.

"Hey, it's my love, birdies," Tony said to them with a grin. "What would you like to have today?"

Graydon and Sophie looked at each other and then back at Tony. "The usual, two Cappuccinos, please," Graydon declared enthusiastically. "We have to celebrate."

As Tony made their drinks, he did so with an amused yet nonchalant look. "Well, well, well," he exclaimed, a wide smile spreading. "What's the occasion?" He asked while serving their favorite coffee drinks to the blissful couple. Graydon grabbed them from him, and he and Sophie grinned, looking at each other. "We're getting married!" they announced together as he took and kissed her left hand.

For them, this news was their life's single most important one. Tony's eyes widened in delight at the news as well. "Ha! I made a note to myself the first night you met this would happen," he said with admiration. "That's wonderful news! Congratulations, you two!" He shook Graydon's hand and leaned in to hug Sophie. "When's the big day?"

Graydon and Sophie exchanged a knowing glance. "As soon as possible! We'll let you know the date after we iron out all the details."

Tony popped the cork from his best bubbly and proposed a toast, "Here's to love, laughter, and happily ever after!"

Graydon and Sophie raised their flutes in unison. Their eyes were locked in a silent promise to each other. "To love, laughter, and happily ever after," they echoed. The words carried the weight of their shared dreams and aspirations.

***

"Why am I the lucky one chosen to write these checks every year?" Sophie quipped with playful sarcasm as she glanced at Graydon, who stood beside her, sifting through the papers.

Sophie sat at the kitchen table as the crisp April morning sun streamed through the window. Today was April 15th, and their annual tax paperwork needed to be filed. Two folders lay before her, marked "IRS" and "State."

Graydon chuckled and took her hand in his. "Because your dad hesitated when I asked for his permission to marry you," he replied, romanticizing the boring task at hand.

Sophie couldn't help but laugh at Graydon's response. A fond smile tugged at her lips. "He was only trying to protect me," she added wittily, squinting her eyes and reflecting her affection as she reached out to squeeze Graydon's hand.

***

Graydon and Sophie decided to visit her parents the weekend before her twenty-fifth birthday, two weeks after their toast with Tony. They had discussed how their parents would react to an engagement just six months after they met. When they arrived, Sophie's mother quickly took her aside. Her eyes were sparkling with curiosity.

"When's the wedding?" she whispered with anticipation.

Her mother's question took Sophie aback, and her cheeks flushed with surprise. "Mom! Where's that coming from?" she exclaimed. Her heart raced at the question. Her mother smiled knowingly. "The way he looks at you. It's deep. It's from his soul. And you, your face has never been brighter. Both of you, your eyes give it away."

Sophie's heart swelled with emotion, and she felt tears forming as her mother spoke. "What about Dad? Will he notice?" she asked. Her mother nodded with a knowing smile gracing her lips. "He should. But he won't. I'll ask him later tonight. I'm guessing Graydon wants his permission?" Sophie bowed her head and nodded as she dried her tears.

***

Sophie was born and raised in a ski resort town in the mountains of Colorado. Her parents were Scandinavians who immigrated when relatives from Germany, who ran a popular resort in one of Bavaria's most idyllic regions, decided to obtain property in the United States. They helped build and establish a quaint inn on land at the mountain's base with plenty of room to expand. Her father was the resort's property manager. He worked diligently to ensure the facilities were managed as a world-class hotel. Her mother assisted the resort's staff manager, but her children were always her top priority. Nothing in life was more important than her family.

Sophie's childhood was a perfect blend of discipline and fun. She and her two older brothers were instilled with a deep admiration and appreciation for God's creation that surrounded them. Living in the mountains provided many exciting adventures for the siblings. There was skiing in the winter and mountain biking in the summer, and there were plenty of activities to participate in around town. They made friends easily, and the people in the community made them feel at home. Sophie's parents made sure that their children always felt loved and valued. They worked hard to provide the means to secure their children's success.

***

"Well, of course, you have our blessing," Sophie's father replied when Graydon asked for her hand. With a proud smile, handshake, and slap on the back, he added, "We're thrilled to have you in our family." Her mother asked, "Do you have a date and location in mind? I can't wait to get the planning started!"

Although her parents did not set a budget, Sophie was very frugal. She and Graydon both wanted to avoid excessive expenses for the wedding. An evening ceremony followed by a lavish dinner would be very costly. On top of that, getting to the airport and their honeymoon destination at a reasonable hour was their priority. An afternoon ceremony on a brisk autumn day would be perfect.

Six months later, the wedding was held at the charming non-denominational church her family had faithfully attended for many years. They kept the ceremony small and intimate, inviting less than a hundred of their closest friends and family. A coffee and cake reception at the church followed the 2:00 P.M. ceremony.

A few minutes before 4:00 P.M., Sophie's godfather, George Metcalf, congratulated them as they prepared to leave the reception, "Congratulations, you two. I know a great journey lies ahead. Graydon, you know I'm an attorney specializing in banking and securities, so don't hesitate to track me down if you ever need advice." he said with a wink and nod. "Will do, Mr. Metcalf," Graydon said as he shook his hand. To everyone's surprise, except the happy couple who had pre-arranged their departure, a helicopter appeared and landed in the adjoining park. The happy couple hugged their parents and thanked them for providing such a beautiful wedding day. As they boarded the helicopter, Sophie and Graydon waved goodbye to their families and wedding guests, grinning at each other as they lifted off to the first adventure of their married life.

***

On that day, just as the evening they first met, Sophie became his partner in every way possible. Even in his breakthrough moment when he decided to act on his ETF idea, Sophie stood and supported him. From the MBS modeling to forming ETFs that challenged the norms of the financial industry, Sophie offered her expert advice.

With his innovative approach to investment management, Graydon believed that ETFs could be a significant change for the fund. However, he also recognized that penetrating the regulatory settings of the firm could be challenging. Fortunately, he was undeterred by the bureaucratic hurdles. He understood that the Securities and Exchange Commission (SEC) ETF Advisor application process was complex but relatively straightforward for those who could afford to cover the required legal and setup fees.

With this sharp vision, Graydon set about completing the necessary paperwork. During this process, Sophie tracked each detail, ensuring he was not missing any detail needed. Thus, he fulfilled the governing requirements to become an SEC-approved ETF Advisor. He knew this was imperative to democratize capitalizing and expanding the fund's reach. Graydon remained focused on the ultimate goal as he moved on with the application process. He needed to provide investors with access to advanced asset prospects. This way, rapid growth for the stakeholders was possible. He was ready to become the latest prodigy of Wall Street.

Chapter 9: Success

The THF office felt like a second home to Graydon. He had developed into a key figure in the company over the years, well-known for his astute financial sense and proficiency with intricate market techniques— especially when it came to ETFs. As proof of his esteemed leadership, the office walls were lined with an impressive collection of charts, graphs, and framed memorabilia from the various business events he'd attended.

With Graydon's prolific mindset, he had accomplished quite an illustrious career in a short time but still had dreams to fulfill. He was captivated by a thought that had taken root in his mind. Though it began as a whisper, it grew louder every day: it was time to bring the dream he'd shared with his parents to reality.

One evening, after his coworkers had all left, Graydon sat at his desk and gazed out his office window at the city's skyline. He knew he had to talk to Sophie before making any plans. Thus, he planned to surprise her with his news over dinner.

Shortly after he arrived home, he was in the kitchen working with a medium saucepan of pasta sauce, letting it gently simmer on a low setting. The aroma of tomatoes and herbs filled the room. He knew that tonight was the night to share his plans with Sophie. He had been trying to make this decision for months and was finally ready. As he set the sauce aside, Sophie walked in. Her eyes brightened, and her smile widened as she sniffed the air. "Smells amazing," she said, leaning in to give him a quick kiss on the cheek. "What's the occasion?"

Graydon took a deep breath as mixed feelings of excitement and nervousness crossed his chest. He'd been rehearsing this conversation in his mind for weeks, but now that the moment had come, he was overwhelmed. "Yes, actually," he replied, taking her hand and leading her to the dining table. "There's something I want to talk to you about."

Sophie's expression shifted to one of curiosity. "What is it?" she asked, sitting down across from him. She could sense that this wasn't just an ordinary dinner. Something significant was on his mind. Graydon gathered his thoughts as he began, "I've been thinking about what we've talked about before. You know, about me, us, starting our own firm. Taking the skills and knowledge we've gained and putting them to use for ourselves," he said with passion. "I'm ready. Are you ready to take the leap of faith?"

"Graydon, that's amazing," she said while reaching out to hold his hand. "I'm so proud of you. I knew this day would come." He clasped her hand as her reaction filled him with relief and gratitude. "Are you sure?" he asked, wanting to be certain that she was as ready for this new chapter as he was. Her opinion always mattered as it seemed she always knew what was best. "It'll be a big change, and there's risk involved, but I'm sure. I believe in you, and I know you'll make it work. Besides, she added with a playful grin, I'll finally get to see you do your own thing instead of just hearing about it."

Graydon laughed as he felt a weight lift off his shoulders. "Yeah, it's about time, isn't it?" he said. "I've been talking about this for ages, haven't I?"

Sophie nodded. "You've got the skills, the drive, and the vision. And you've got me in your corner," she said. "We'll do this together." Through her words, Graydon felt a surge of confidence. As they sat down to enjoy their dinner, the night felt charged with possibility. Graydon was ready to take the next step, and he knew that with Sophie's support, they would be unstoppable.

***

Their apartment felt smaller as Graydon looked around the living room, which was now filled with stacks of folders and various ringed binders. Presently, several papers and books were spread out in a semi-circle around him. His laptop buzzed quietly on the coffee table, and notifications blinked to remind him of the pressing deadlines that loomed ahead. Sophie was out with friends for the evening, leaving him to focus on the task of completing applications to secure capital for their new venture.

Ever since he started at THF, he has been building savings. A portion of each month's pay, along with every bonus, had gone back to Citizens First Bank and entered his childhood savings account. It was far more than enough to cover the initial costs of setting up the business infrastructure and legal fees. But it wasn't enough to launch the ETF he'd been planning. For that, he'd need outside investors and or a business loan.

Graydon took a deep breath and leaned back against the couch. He was simultaneously exhilarated and exhausted by the effort. The struggle to this point had been demanding, with long nights and struggling to arrange meetings with potential investors.

He'd started with his closest connections, like his friends from the other firms and their contacts who knew of his reputation. All of them had been willing to invest small amounts, enough to show their support but not enough to fund the whole project.

"Graydon, this is great, but I'm not in a position to go all in," said Vance, his early morning friend from THF who'd moved back to his family's office in California. "After you get more traction, we can chip in, but right now, it's too early for us."

"No problem, I understand," Graydon replied, keeping his disappointment in check. "Thanks for considering it. I'll keep you updated on how it goes."

His next step was to approach more substantial investors. This included people with deep pockets and a higher risk tolerance. It wasn't an easy sell to them as they would require a substantial equity piece to offset the lack of experience from a young professional with a new business idea that would test the market's appetite.

During one particularly nerve-wracking meeting, he sat across from a group of venture capitalists in a sleek boardroom. The lead investor, a stern-looking woman named Karen, spoke up in a critical tone, "You've got an interesting concept, Graydon, but why should we invest in your ETF when there are dozens of other established funds out there? What makes yours different?"

Graydon's palms were sweating slightly. He cleared his throat and began, "My ETF focuses on an innovative approach to asset management, particularly mortgage-backed securities, using a blend of traditional strategies and emerging technology. I'm confident that this approach will be successful and attract not only traditional investors but also those new to the markets."

Karen didn't look entirely convinced, but she nodded. "All right, we'll think about it. Some of the team may reach out with questions. We'll decide within two weeks."

In the meantime, Graydon applied for a business loan via a contact given to him by Mr. Hopkins, as First Citizens Bank was always focused on local lending. The process was tedious, with endless paperwork and follow-up back-and-forth with bank representatives. At the same time he received their approval email earlier that day, granting him enough capital to cover the ETF's launch, Karen called to outline their proposed terms before extending their offer. He asked if they could be sent via email and that he would reply within a few days.

Now, as he sat among the paperwork in his living room, Graydon felt relieved. The pieces were coming together. The small investors, the loan, and his savings were enough to get started. He'd made it through the initial hurdles, and the path ahead seemed a bit clearer.

Just then, Sophie entered the apartment with a smile on her face. "Hey, how's it going?" she asked, noticing the spread of papers.

Graydon looked up, a grin breaking across his face. "I got the loan approval," he said, unable to contain his excitement. "We're set. We can launch the ETF."

Sophie rushed over, hugging him tightly. "That's amazing! I knew you could do it," she shrieked. "I'm so proud of you,

Graydon." Graydon hugged her back, his heart swelling with gratitude.

* * *

Graydon had spent months immersed in the intricacies of regulatory compliance. The meetings with legal experts and late-night review sessions had left him exhausted yet energized. Successfully navigating this terrain meant culminating in the launch of his ETF.

The day before the official launch, Graydon sat in a final meeting with his compliance team, double-checking every detail to ensure they had met all the Securities and Exchange Commission (SEC) requirements.

"Are we confident the prospectus is solid?" Graydon asked, looking around the table. The team nodded, but Graydon could sense the tension. No one wanted to miss a critical detail that could jeopardize the launch. "Good. Let's make sure we stay on top of any changes in the regulations. The last thing we need is to be caught off guard."

Later that evening, Graydon returned to his apartment to find Sophie waiting with a celebratory dinner.

"How did it go today?" she asked, handing him a flute.

"All good," Graydon replied, taking a sip. "The team is confident we're ready for tomorrow. But I'm still a little nervous."

Sophie laughed softly. "Of course you are. It's a big deal. But you've worked so hard for this, and I know it's going to be amazing."

Graydon nodded, feeling the warmth of her support. "Thanks. I don't think I could have done it without you."

The day of the ETF launch arrived, and Graydon felt excitement and anxieties coursing through his veins. Months of arduous work made it possible to bring his innovative ETF to market. Graydon arrived at the firm's office early. The team gathered in the conference room for a final briefing, and Graydon addressed them.

"Today is a big day for all of us," he said, looking around at his colleagues. "We've put in the work, and now it's time to see the results. Let's make sure we stay focused and handle any issues that come our way."

The launch event was held in a modern conference room. A large screen displayed the logo of Graydon's firm alongside the name of the new ETF: "InnovateX." Rows of chairs filled the room, and investors, colleagues, and members of the financial community were gathered with anticipation.

The room fell silent as he began his presentation, outlining the vision and strategy behind "InnovateX." He spoke with passion and conviction, sharing his insights into the market and the unique value proposition of the ETF.

"Our goal with 'InnovateX' is to provide investors with a channel for accessing companies across various sectors. Our ETF promises to revolutionize the way investors engage with the stock market." Graydon explained in a steady and confident tone. Throughout the presentation, Graydon easily fielded questions from the audience, addressing concerns and providing clarity on the fund's objectives and investment approach. The response from stockholders was overwhelmingly positive, with many expressing interest in allocating capital to InnovateX.

Following the presentation, Graydon mingled with attendees, shaking hands and exchanging business cards. Sophie stood by his side with her ever-radiant smile of pride and support.

"You did it, Graydon," she said with admiration. "I'm so proud of you." Graydon squeezed her hand as a sense of accomplishment washed over him. "We did it," he replied with gratitude.

It took only a few days for Graydon's ETF to take the market by storm. Every day, the volume of trades involving his ETF grew, and its value climbed steadily. Industry analysts began talking about it, and financial news outlets highlighted it as a star performer, comparing its growth to those of more established funds. One of Graydon's ETFs was a collection of bank and financial service companies that have been outperforming the markets. This meant more investors were purchasing the ETF, causing the ETF to purchase more shares of the collection.

Mid-morning, two weeks after the launch, Graydon answered his phone. "Hello, Graydon, this is Tom Harvey with the NYSE. We'd like you to come here and ring the opening bell in three weeks. Are you interested?"

✳✳✳

Mid-afternoon, two weeks after ringing the bell, Graydon heard his phone and noticed the caller ID display "Bolt Bank." He was curious as he hadn't had any direct contact with them before. He answered the call, and his tone was friendly but professional. "Hello, this is Graydon."

"Good morning, Graydon," came the voice on the other end. It was smooth and calm. "This is Rebecca from Bolt Bank Holding Company. Mr. Arnold would like to meet you at his office. Are you available around 3:00 P.M. tomorrow?"

What could Mr. Arnold, one of the most influential figures in the region's banking industry, want with him? Was this a business opportunity? A possible partnership? Or something else entirely? The uncertainty added an edge to his voice as he replied.

"Of course," he said, keeping his voice steady. "I'll be there."

"Thank you," Rebecca responded. "We look forward to seeing you."

Graydon felt a perplexed trepidation about the meeting. That evening, Sophie noticed his distraction and asked, "What's going on? You seem a bit off."

"I got a call from Bolt Bank Holding Company," He informed her. "They want me to meet with Mr. Arnold."

Sophie raised an eyebrow. "That's interesting. What do you think it's about?"

"I have no idea," he said, still processing the call. "It could be a good thing, but I'm not sure. They're known for aggressive business tactics."

"Well, be careful," Sophie said with evident concern. "Don't consider anything without praying and thinking it through."

Graydon nodded, his mind already working through possible scenarios. Whatever Mr. Arnold had in mind, Graydon knew he'd need to be on his toes. The financial world was full of twists and turns, and a meeting with someone like Mr. Arnold could signal an opportunity or a threat. He just hoped it was the former and not the latter.

Chapter 10: The Shadow of Greed

"I am not about to allow Graydon Maxwell's ETF to become one of our largest shareholders," Mr. Arnold mumbled to himself as he reviewed his company's quarterly shareholder report. The numbers had left him with a bitter taste in his mouth. He was in his expansive office. The walls of the room were lined with portraits of past family members and industry accolades. His desk was a grand piece of mahogany furniture that seemed to stretch across the room and was littered with papers and reports.

Mr. Arnold placed the report back on his desk. He stood up, pushing his chair back with a hint of impatience, and walked over to the large window that dominated one entire wall of his office. The view stretched across the city skyline that stretched into the distance. As he stood there, looking out at the bustling city below, a sense of unease settled over him. This was his domain, the empire he'd built and maintained for decades. He wasn't about to let anyone disrupt the balance of power. His reflection in the window looked back at him. The deep lines on his face hardened with a solemn frown.

Mr. Arnold was a formidable figure in the banking world. At nearly 75 years old, he had weathered decades of economic booms and busts. His influence grew with each passing year. His bank, the flagship of Bolt Bank Holding Company, was a multi-generational family-owned and operated holding company known as the most successful in the region.

They had gone public only a few years earlier, not out of necessity but for strategic reasons. The move allowed them to consolidate several different banks they owned under one name. This simplified estate planning and helped the family avoid hefty taxation. Mr. Arnold saw the public offering as a necessary means to an end, validating his irrefutable reputation for getting what he wanted.

Mr. Arnold's presence was as imposing as his reputation. He stood at an impressive six-foot-four, with grey hair and dark eyes that seemed to pierce through anything or anyone. He moved with a calculated swagger, and his steps were slow and deliberate, as if each had been planned. His voice was deep and authoritative, carrying the weight of someone accustomed to being listened to without question. Despite his age, Mr. Arnold retained a sharp intellect, and his dominating influence in the banking world carried a lot of clout.

The cityscape seemed to sway slightly in the light, causing the skyscrapers to shine. He felt a trace of vertigo in the sky as he tightened his grip on the window ledge. It was a fleeting sensation, but it reminded him that stability in the banking world was often an illusion. He knew that those who weren't vigilant could find themselves at the mercy of forces beyond their control.

He took a deep breath, his chest rising and falling with slow deliberation. He turned away from the window and walked back to his desk. The report lay open, and he glared at it once again. He slowly rubbed his temples, concentrating his thoughts on the strategies he could devise.

Mr. Arnold incorporated every scheme and tactic available to gain success. He employed any plot that could accelerate his success, even if it meant playing in gray areas. When he saw an opportunity to manipulate for profit, he did not let it pass by.

He had recently been acquiring smaller banks struggling with the latest round of burdensome regulations, offering them an opportunity to walk away before their profitability shrank further. These deals often came with strict terms that favored his interests well into the future. By consolidating these banks under the Bolt name, he created an appearance of stability and growth, attracting investors who didn't look too closely at the apparent hints.

Mr. Arnold also had a knack for using complex financial instruments to his advantage. Whether it was restructuring assets to reduce tax liabilities or selling loan participations with wide margins, he knew how to make the most out of others' weaknesses. He constantly pushed auditors to use creative accounting techniques to present the most favorable view of his financial statements, often stretching the truth to maintain investor confidence.

Gradually, his influence extended to the higher authority as well. He cultivated relationships with important politicians and lobbyists, contributing to their campaigns and using his connections to shape financial regulations in ways that benefited his company. He used his network to smoothly deal with potential issues through his friendship card or to gain early access to information that could give him an edge in the market.

On the operations side, Mr. Arnold was known for his aggressive cost-cutting strategies. He reduced overhead by outsourcing jobs to lower-cost regions and automating processes whenever possible. Employee benefits and wages were often the first targets.

In his dealings with clients and other businesses, Mr. Arnold was adept at manipulating contracts to ensure he always came out ahead. He used hidden fees, complex terms, and one-sided clauses to extract maximum value from every deal. If a partner or client found themselves in a tight spot, Mr. Arnold didn't hesitate to use it to his advantage, pushing for more favorable terms or additional concessions.

His approach to business was ruthless but effective. Under his leadership, Bolt Bank Holding Company grew from a small regional bank to a major player in the region. He believed that in the business world, it was the merciless who prospered, and he was determined to stay at the top, no matter what it took.

It was only a few months back that he learned about this young man in the field who was being called a prodigy. One typical day, Mr. Arnold was at the head of the long conference table, surrounded by his team of senior and junior executives. He heard one of the junior employees talking before the meeting commenced.

"Did you see how Graydon Maxwell left THF and has his own company? He has some really advanced strategies. He suggests ETFs as a route to allow the general public to invest and take advantage of the same benefits as wealthy clients."

Mr. Arnold overheard the comment and scoffed inwardly. *'How foolish and childish!'* he thought, dismissing the notion as imbecile. *'These new kids know nothing better. They think they can take on the world with some innovative ideas. Imagine ETF being the way to advantage!'* he continued to muse. *'And even if it is, just think of it! Why would you allow the general public to benefit the same as the wealthy ones? What profit is in that?'*

In his lengthy career, he'd seen countless young upstarts try to make a name for themselves. They came and went, their motivations quickly fading as the harsh realities of the business world took their toll. He had seen it all before—young entrepreneurs who believed they could revolutionize the industry but ultimately crumbled under pressure.

However, after only a few days, his curiosity was piqued when he heard another senior executive casually mention, "Graydon Maxwell just launched his ETF, InnovateX, and it includes an allocation in our shares. He's a prodigy for sure."

This caught Mr. Arnold off guard. He had underestimated the reach of this young man, and now, his name was circulating among his senior team. There was suddenly a spark in Mr. Arnold's mind as he heard the name again. He instinctively went online and typed in 'Graydon Maxwell.' The search engine immediately displayed several current news articles and reports, with Graydon's face appearing at the top of the screen. The more he read, the more intrigued he became.

It seemed that Graydon had done more than just launch a promising ETF. His approach, as he had heard his junior employee say, was unique and focused on allowing a broader range of investors to access financial markets typically dominated by the wealthy. His concept was gaining traction, and his accomplishment was undeniable.

Never did he imagine the concept was a wave but an ocean current. As the days turned into weeks, it became clear that InnovateX was gaining momentum, attracting investors from all walks of life, and earning a reputation for its solid performance. The young man was challenging the status quo, and his influence was spreading. It was no longer possible to ignore him. Mr. Arnold knew that he needed to keep a close watch on this rising star, for his success could have far-reaching implications. The winds of change were blowing, and Mr. Arnold was determined to stay ahead of the storm.

Seven weeks after the launch, while he sat in his office, reviewing shareholder reports, Mr. Arnold could not believe what started as a tiny spark had ignited a fire. InnovateX was on the verge of becoming one of the largest shareholders and was in a position to demand a seat on the Board of Directors.

"Impossible," he mumbled to himself, tossing the report onto the desk with a flick of his wrist. The crumpled pages slid across the smooth surface, stopping just before the edge. He stood up and walked to the large window once again. The world he'd shaped for himself was now being challenged by a young man with radical ideas about democratizing finance.

Graydon unknowingly became a direct threat to this traditional yet underhanded banking operations. If his influence took hold, it would undermine Mr. Arnold's control over regional banking matters, including public deposits, disrupting everything Mr. Arnold had spent decades establishing.

He considered his next move. Maxwell had never been on his radar, but now InnovateX's stake was growing too large for comfort. He hastily pressed a button on his telecom phone and buzzed his secretary, who, as was always the case, answered on the first ring.

"Rebecca," he said on the speakerphone. "Yes, sir." She replied promptly from the other side.

"Please come to my office," he commanded.

Rebecca arrived almost immediately, with her footsteps quick and efficient. She entered the office with a notepad in hand. Her demeanor was respectful yet confident. "How can I assist you, Mr. Arnold?" she asked, noticing the tension in his expression.

"Call Graydon Maxwell," he said, not bothering to hide his frustration. "I want him in my office for a meeting. Tomorrow, if possible."

Rebecca nodded as her pen poised to take notes. "Do you have a specific time in mind?"

"As soon as he can get here," he replied, his eyes still fixed on the cityscape. "Tell him it's urgent."

Rebecca wrote down the instructions, then paused. "Would you like me to give him any specific reason for the meeting?"

Mr. Arnold turned to face her, his gaze steady and stern. "Just tell him it's in his best interest."

Rebecca nodded, her expression remaining neutral. "Understood, sir. I'll contact him immediately and let you know once he's confirmed the time."

"Thank you, Rebecca," he said, dismissing her with a wave of his hand.

Chapter 11: Conspiracy

Graydon was sitting outside Mr. Arnold's office just before 3:00 P.M. He was a stickler for punctuality and assumed the same held true for Mr. Arnold. The office lobby was busy, filled with the murmur of employees and the ringing of phones. Graydon tried to focus on the news magazine in his hands, but his mind kept racing back to the purpose of this urgent meeting. He was nervously tapping his foot while staring at the wall clock in front of him. *What could Mr. Arnold want from him? Why did he ask him to meet him so urgently? Was he in some kind of trouble?* The thoughts ran rampant in his mind as he looked around.

The office lobby was a lustrous, modern space designed to impress. Polished marble floors reflected the soft glow of recessed lighting, creating a smooth sheen that stretched across the expansive area. Large windows along one side allowed natural light to pour in, offering a panoramic view of the bustling city streets below.

The reception desk was a long, curved structure made of dark mahogany with a glossy finish. Behind it, the receptionist worked efficiently, her fingers tapping quickly on the keyboard as she answered calls and directed visitors. She had a friendly demeanor, but her movements were precise and purposeful, indicative of the fast-paced environment.

The walls were adorned with contemporary art and abstract pieces that added pops of color to the otherwise neutral tones of the lobby. A few strategically placed potted plants brought a touch of greenery. Their leaves stood out against the clean lines of the architecture.

A few comfortable leather chairs that appeared to have never been sat in were next to the windows. A low coffee table stood in the center, stacked with industry magazines and business journals. The buzz of activity throughout the building created a vivid atmosphere. In one corner, a small refreshment station offered snacks, tea, and water. The coffee machine emitted a soft whirring sound as it brewed a fresh cup. The aroma of roasted coffee beans subtly permeated the air.

"Mr. Maxwell?" she called out, breaking his train of thought. He didn't respond immediately, lost in his concerns about what Mr. Arnold might want.

"Graydon Maxwell?" she repeated, her voice a bit louder this time.

Graydon snapped out of his thoughts and lifted his hand, a bit embarrassed for not reacting sooner. "Yes," he said, trying to smile despite his nervousness.

"Mr. Arnold will see you now," the receptionist informed him. Her voice was polite but firm. Graydon quickly put the magazine down and stood up. "Thank you," he said, feeling awkward for raising his hand earlier. He straightened his tie and walked toward the large door leading to Mr. Arnold's office.

Mr. Arnold looked up as Graydon entered. His eyes were sharp and assessing. Despite his reputation for being stern, his expression softened as he greeted Graydon with a smile. "Ah, Mr. Maxwell. Please, please come in," he said in a cordial and welcoming tone.

Graydon stepped forward, feeling the warmth of the greeting but still anxious about the meeting's purpose. "Thank you, it's nice to meet you, Mr. Arnold," he replied.

"Of course, of course," Mr. Arnold said as he shook his hand and gestured to an excessively padded chair opposite his desk. "Please, have a seat."

Graydon nodded and took the seat, but his movements were slightly tense. He felt swallowed by the chair as he tried to relax, but the apprehensive thoughts churning in his mind made it difficult. The room was quiet, and the only sound came from the ticking of a clock on the wall.

Mr. Arnold leaned back in his chair, steepling his fingers as he studied Graydon. "So, how are things with you?" he asked. His voice was conversational now but with a subtle edge of curiosity.

Graydon cleared his throat, trying to keep his response casual. "They're going well, thank you," he replied, hoping to keep the conversation light.

"Yes, I've heard," Mr. Arnold said with a slight smile tugging at the corners of his lips. "You've made quite a name for yourself in a very short amount of time. Impressive, considering how young you are."

Graydon felt a surge of pride but quickly suppressed it. "Thank you. It's nice to see some fruit from my hard work."

Mr. Arnold nodded with his expression thoughtful. "Indeed. Hard work and a bit of luck here and there is a potent combination. But it's also about timing and understanding the broader picture." He leaned forward with an intense gaze. "I'm sure you're wondering why I called you in today, Mr. Maxwell," Mr. Arnold began with a smooth and deep tone. "Well, I'm a fan of your work. The way you turned your ETF into a top investment product in such a brief time is commendable." He offered a genuine smile, a rarity for the otherwise stoic banker.

Graydon felt a cautious optimism. It wasn't every day that a high-ranking figure like Mr. Arnold complimented his work. "Thank you," he replied, keeping his tone respectful but professional. "It's been quite a journey, made better over the last few years by my wife and children."

Mr. Arnold blinked, acknowledging Graydon's words before continuing. "I called you here today because I know that your ETF is a collection of our bank and financial service companies, and it's been outperforming the market, evenly comprised of 25 bank holding companies located in the central region of the United States. Their performance has exceeded those on the East and West coasts. That's remarkable, Graydon."

Graydon listened intently, wondering where this conversation was heading. It was rare for a man like Mr. Arnold to call a meeting without a clear agenda, and he had a knack for getting straight to the point.

"So," Mr. Arnold said, leaning forward, "I have an offer for you that I believe you can't resist." He paused for dramatic effect, watching Graydon's reaction.

Graydon raised an eyebrow as his interest piqued. "I'm listening," he said, keeping his tone neutral.

Mr. Arnold continued, "I'd like to purchase your ETF and take complete ownership of it. In return, I'm willing to offer you a substantial sum. How does $20 million sound?" Mr. Arnold said, leaning back in his chair with a confident smile. "And we will hire you as investment CEO to shape our entire investment strategy with a contract that includes additional bonuses and perks. It's a win-win."

Graydon's heart pounded as he processed the offer. $20 million was an astounding amount, more than he'd ever imagined having in their bank account this early in his career. It was the kind of money that could change his life in an instant. He could buy property, invest in other ventures, and lock down a comfortable future for himself, Sophie, and their children. The allure of the offer was strong, and he could feel the weight of the decision pressing down on him.

However, as he looked into Mr. Arnold's eyes, he could sense an underlying expectation, the assumption that everyone had a price and Graydon's price had just been named. It was tempting, undeniably so, but he couldn't ignore the feeling in his gut that told him to hold his ground. He remembered Sophie's beautiful face and how she cautioned him to make a wise decision.

Thus, with a deep breath, keeping his composure, he replied. "That's a generous offer, Mr. Arnold, and I appreciate it. But I have a vision for my ETF, and I'm not ready to let it go. I believe it can make a significant impact in the financial world, and I want to see that through."

Mr. Arnold's smile faded, and his eyes narrowed in such a manner that Graydon didn't see any light in his eyes, just a dark, soul-piercing glare. "I understand your passion, Mr. Maxwell, but opportunities like this don't come along every day. You'd be foolish to pass it up. Think of what you could do with such an exorbitant amount of money."

Graydon nodded, acknowledging the gravity of the offer. "It is a lot to pass on, but at this point, I need to stay true to my vision." Deep down, he knew he had built their company and InnovateX on the principles of accessibility and fairness. Selling it to a large bank holding company would immediately compromise those principles.

Mr. Arnold's expression grew stern, his patience worn thin. "Very well," he said as his tone lost all of its warmth. "I hope you realize what you're turning down, Mr. Maxwell. This is a one-time offer. Once it's off the table, there's no coming back!" He annunciated the last sentence a little too deeply, emphasizing that this meant enmity with him. It was a warning that if Graydon did not take the offer, it would mean he was against Mr. Arnold and would be treated like a foe.

However, Graydon held his ground, and his resolve remained unshaken. "I understand, Mr. Arnold. Thank you for the opportunity, but I have to decline."

The room fell silent as Mr. Arnold regarded him with a hard stare. It was clear that he wasn't accustomed to hearing the word "no," especially not from someone as young as Graydon. However, Graydon knew what he had done and was willing to face the consequences of his decision, although none came to mind.

Mr. Arnold managed to maintain his composure. "Very well," he said, his tone carefully controlled. "I respect your decision." With that, Graydon rose from his seat and exited.

"I will show him." Mr. Arnold muttered behind him as Graydon left his office.

***

Jay Willard, a nearby banker who originated the Maxwell's loan to purchase the securities firm, looked at the caller ID display as he picked up his phone and said, "Mr. Arnold, what a pleasant surprise to hear from you. What can I do for you?" Jay's son was being groomed to replace him upon his retirement, and as is the norm in the banking community, he was working for Mr. Arnold to gain experience outside of their bank.

"I've met your son on a couple of occasions and have been told he's doing a nice job for us," Mr. Arnold replied. "However, I'm calling today to talk about Graydon Maxwell. He's quickly established a nice company, but he's gone too far, too fast with his ETFs."

"Too far, too fast?" Jay repeated, confused by the statement. "I'm not sure I understand."

"When he first bought the securities firm, I was told you originated his loan. I assume you still have it. I thought you should know he may have a few questions pop up in the very near future from the state regulators, and you should be preparing to respond."

The revelation struck Jay like a cold blast of arctic air. Perplexed at Mr. Arnold's statement, he replied, "Oh, my. I'm shocked to hear that. I didn't see that coming. I've known his parents for over 20 years and watched him grow up," he said, trying to process the unexpected warning.

"Oh, by the way," Mr. Arnold continued casually, "we're hosting a reception for the newly elected state representatives next Thursday at 4:00 P.M. You should plan to attend." A wicked smile tugged at Mr. Arnold's lips as he suddenly changed the topic, trying to allure Mr. Willard.

"Okay, sir. I'll plan to be there, for sure. Thanks for your call," Jay gratefully replied. It was as if Mr. Arnold's trap had been successful, and without thinking much, Mr. Jay had been prey.

As soon as the call ended, Jay's thoughts raced. He immediately reached for his phone and dialed his attorney. "I just received a call out of the blue from Mike Arnold. The gist of it was to inform me that Graydon Maxwell may have an issue with state regulators. Your thoughts?" he asked in an urgent tone.

The attorney paused, clearly caught off guard by the news. "Oh, I need to walk down the hall and check with the other banking law partners. I've not heard of anything, but if Arnold called, something's in the works. I'll call back shortly."

Jay hung up and turned to his computer, tapping away on the keyboard to pull up the Maxwell Companies folder. The financial records showed that Mr. and Mrs. Maxwell each held 50% of the company, which started with the purchase of the securities firm and grew with the creation of the ETF Advisor and the mortgage underwriter. The most recent audits indicated continued growth and profitability, with steady revenue streams from all three divisions.

An hour went by, and just as Jay was about to call his attorney again, his phone rang. It was his attorney, calling back with news. "I don't have enough information to share at this point, but I'd like to meet with you offsite early next week. Perhaps a late breakfast on Tuesday?" he suggested.

"Okay. Let's meet at Eggscetera at 9:30 A.M.," Jay replied, feeling the weight of the situation. The uncertainty was unnerving, and he knew that when Mr. Arnold raised concerns, it was rarely without cause.

The call ended, and Jay leaned back in his chair, the worn leather creaking beneath him. The warning from Mr. Arnold could have serious implications. He couldn't help but feel a sense of responsibility to get to the bottom of this. But for now, he had to wait and see what the attorney could tell him. He wasn't ready to be caught in the crossfire of whatever was brewing.

Chapter 12: Betrayal Unfolds

Mr. Willard had spent the nights since his last conversation with his attorney tossing and turning, unable to sleep. He kept wondering what it could mean if Mr. Arnold decided to lean on him. He knew this wouldn't be an easy fix, and the uncertainty was gnawing at him. Tuesday finally came, and as he entered the small breakfast diner, the fresh coffee and sizzling bacon greeted him with its aroma. It would have been comforting under other circumstances, but it only made him more anxious today. He spotted his attorney in a far corner booth and reached him.

"Good morning," Mr. Willard said as he slid into the booth.

"Well, it's not," his attorney replied, not even attempting to mask his grim expression. "Jay, simply put, Arnold is about to lean on you. I hope we can work together and keep you upright. Hopefully, none the worse for wear."

Mr. Willard sighed, trying to keep his composure. "I'm guessing this is the point at which I just sit and listen. So, tell me the story while I try to enjoy my last supper, so to speak, in the form of their signature waffle."

His attorney nodded, understanding the gravity of the situation. "Arnold has decided Maxwell is moving too far, too fast.," he began, his voice low. "They've only met once, but Arnold was intimidated by his youth, broad intellect, and moral compass. You might recall there have been several deals Maxwell wouldn't underwrite or participate in because, as was reported back to Arnold, he didn't think they passed the 'smell test.' He expressly told those involved that he would not have his name associated with Arnold in any manner."

Mr. Willard nodded, recalling conversations with Graydon about his business principles. "Yeah, I remember those deals. I asked him about it a while back, and he reminded me that he and his wife are 50/50 in the company. He said they both agreed that he wouldn't get involved in anything or with anyone that might cast a shadow on them. He doesn't need to make every deal. He's developed plenty of other ways to generate additional revenue streams. He's always been well ahead of his repayment schedule."

"Well, aside from those deals, it's also the ETF buying up shares of Bolt that infuriates him," his attorney continued. "No matter that the ETF is bringing positive attention to each company and increasing their value. All Arnold sees is that the ETF keeps buying more of his shares. The third strike was when Arnold quietly tried to buy the securities firm from Maxwell but was turned down."

Mr. Willard now comprehended the reason for Mr. Arnold's anger toward Graydon. He sighed, looking down, and said, "So, Arnold is knocking Maxwell out. How's he planning to do it?"

"Arnold is having the State Securities Department announce an investigation. You know the ink on that will kill Maxwell. You've got his loan, so just after the announcement, go in and tell him to walk away. Arnold will buy it from you. Perhaps he'll move your son over to take charge of the new entity."

Mr. Willard was taken aback. "What happens to the Maxwells?" he asked, concerned about the repercussions for Graydon and his family.

His attorney shrugged, not unsympathetically but with a hint of detachment. "They're young. They can start over. Perhaps you can suggest they move out of state to avoid the fallout."

Mr. Willard shook his head, struggling with the moral implications of what he was being asked to do. "When does this begin?" he asked, feeling the pressure that was about to come down on Graydon.

"On the 8th," his attorney replied.

Mr. Willard's eyes widened. "Wait, they're ringing the bell at the NYSE next Tuesday, the 2nd. A hit that fast will kill the ETFs."

"Exactly. Arnold wants the ETFs to be closed out and liquidated." his attorney said, confirming the ruthless nature of the plan.

"So, on the 9th, I call Maxwell and tell him to come in for a visit?" Mr. Willard asked, trying to confirm the details of his role in this strategy.

"That sounds about right," the attorney replied. "Let's plan to talk the afternoon of the 8th."

Mr. Willard felt the weight of the conversation settling heavily on his shoulders. The stakes were high, and he knew he was being used as a pawn in a larger game of power and influence.

***

The morning of Tuesday the 9th was moving along in its normal fashion, with employees bustling about and Graydon reviewing overnight reports in his office. There was no door as he nurtured an open work environment, always challenging employees to approach him with ideas or suggestions. Complaints were not allowed unless a solution accompanied them.

A new intern on the Trading Desk hesitantly stepped into his office. "Mr. Maxwell, I need to discuss something with you."

Halting his daily routine of numbers crunching, Graydon looked up, "Yes, what is on your mind?"

"I just took a call from a college friend who works at one of the major law firms. He told me during their morning conference, it was mentioned that the State Securities Department's website posted an investigation notice about the brokerage."

Graydon was surprised and perplexed by what he'd just heard. "What? I didn't even know they had a website. In fact, I've never met nor heard from anyone at the State." After the initial shock from the strange news, Graydon decided it must be a case of mistaken identity. There was no reason for the State Securities Department to investigate his brokerage. He thanked the intern for the information and told him not to worry.

Graydon promptly searched for and found the website. On its homepage, he was stunned to see the heading "News," and under it, a hyperlink titled "Order Initiating an Investigation against Maxwell Securities" that was dated and time stamped from the prior afternoon. Curiously, the hyperlink did not work.

Graydon was both confused and shocked. He took a few deep breaths before his mind started churning with possibilities. He had to take someone's advice on this. He began thinking, *'Who to call first? Whom can I call?'* Graydon looked out at the nearby trees and watched their branches wave. He thought to himself, *'The winds of change are blowing.'*

Knowing Sophie was likely busy with their children, he decided he did not want to interrupt her with this news right now. Preferring to tell her face-to-face, he hit the speed dial for their attorney instead.

Joe Nicklas, Maxwell's attorney, was continually amazed at the paths they headed down. Their requests for his work came only after careful thought and with specific instructions. He understood that each step they took was precise and planned. With Graydon and Sophie just back from ringing the bell at NYSE, Mr. Nicklas was surprised when he saw Graydon's number flash on his phone. He answered with, "Hello, Mr. Bell Ringer. You know you're the only person I know who's done that."

Graydon appreciated Joe's kind acknowledgment, saying that today, he did not have precious time to lose with petty conversation. He was direct, "Sorry, Joe, this isn't a pleasant call. I've just been told, and I'm now looking at, an investigation announcement on the State Securities Department website. I'm guessing they've decided to look into why I wouldn't underwrite those tax credit deals last year." Joe was stunned at this sudden revelation.

"What are you talking about? They don't investigate for not doing deals. There's nothing to look at. They also provide a notice when they're about to open an investigation. They've never posted an announcement before presenting a notice." he stated.

"I don't know. I was just informed of this, so I looked it up myself." Graydon explained. "Where are they located? I'm tempted to go to their offices, but I know it's best to get your advice before I do anything." Joe agreed.

Joe took a moment's pause to try to make sense of the situation. "I'll call the administrator as soon as we hang up and get back to you ASAP." Graydon's confidence in his attorney's legal insight gave him the reassurance he needed to feel less anxious. In a few minutes, Graydon's phone buzzed again. He looked at the caller ID; it was Joe. He picked up the phone on the first ring and said, "Well, Joe, what's it to be?"

"Don't know. Not only are you the first to be investigated without receiving notice, but you're also the first to have the lead investigator, the only person who can speak to the notice, out for the rest of the week. I was told I'll receive a call back next week."

Graydon noticed another call lighting up his phone. "Joe, now I've got Jay Willard calling me. I'll call you back."

"Okay, Graydon, weigh your words carefully, and please take care," Joe advised.

"Will do," Graydon assured and switched between the calls, receiving Jay's call. "Hello, Jay."

"Graydon," Jay spoke from the other side in a rushed tone, "I'm sorry to make this call, but I need to ask if you can come to the bank tomorrow morning. If that's not good, perhaps the afternoon?"

Not understanding what it could be that Jay would want, Graydon told him, "Mr. Willard, my calendar for tomorrow is nearly full of conference calls with potentially substantial new investors for the ETFs. Could you stop by here at 9:30 A.M.?"

"Yes, that will work for me. I'll see you then." Jay replied with relief. Then, Graydon disconnected the call with him and called Joe again. When he answered, he informed him, "So, Jay Willard wanted me to come out to his bank tomorrow morning. I told him that wouldn't work with my schedule, so he's coming to my office at 9:30 a.m. Are you available to attend?"

"I'm sorry, I've got tomorrow blocked out with a deposition that's expected to make or break a nearly five-year-old case." Joe regretfully expressed.

Understanding his situation, Graydon responded, "Okay. Well, I'm starting to see the writing on the wall. When I was at Trojan, I heard conversations about circumstances like this. This is a point where you tell friends to forget the business and save the friendship because that's worth more in the long run. I don't want to become a negative to your career and life." Joe thanked him for his thoughtfulness. With that, they ended the call.

***

Jay Willard and several others from his bank waited in the conference room. Graydon finished his call with the Whitestone Group, a large private equity firm that two of his friends from THF now worked for, and then headed to the front conference room. "Good morning, Mr. Willard," he said as he nodded toward the others.

"Graydon, you know Thomas, Betsy, and Larry from the bank," Jay began. "And this is Mr. Tracey, one of our directors. I've been trying to think of how to best begin this conversation. So, I'm just going to start by saying that I became aware of a posting on the State Securities Department's website late Monday afternoon. That's a very serious matter and creates concerns for our bank, given the size of your loan. I'm afraid the impact of an investigation could result in several problems for you and, of course, potential losses for us. We came here this morning to ask you to resign, walk away, and let us take over."

Graydon intentionally paused to make them all even more uncomfortable than he could tell they already were. "Mr. Willard, I have no idea why there's a notice on their website. Whatever they think, I know I haven't done anything wrong. You are aware that we are ahead of schedule on our loan payments. However, I understand why you have concerns about how this so-called investigation could affect the bank. Even though I'm not defaulting on any of the loan's terms, I've already made arrangements to move the loan. You'll be sent a commitment letter no later than tomorrow and, hopefully, be paid off within a week or two."

The color drained from Mr. Willard's face as he struggled to reply. "Okay. Well, we appreciate that. I know you're busy. We'll move on and let you keep at it." Graydon gave the team a sarcastic smile, depicting that he had comprehended their intentions. They all silently got up and left the conference room in a hurry.

Mr. Willard leaned against the building for support immediately after they exited. "I need a few moments to gather my thoughts. That did not go as it was supposed to, and I've got a call I must make that I don't want to make," he said to the others. He pulled out his phone and dialed his attorney.

"Hello, Jay. Did the meeting go as planned?" his attorney asked confidently. "No, it didn't. Maxwell's going to pay us off," his distressed tone was evidence of his fear. The horrors dawned upon him as his mind raced to consider the consequences of what had just happened.

"No way! Oh, no!" his attorney exclaimed. He was just as horrified as Willard. "Nobody thought of that possibility. The managing partners told me to let them know when I hear from you. I've got to go upstairs and report. I doubt you'll hear from me for a while." The long, silent pause before they hung up was a sign that things were about to get ugly.

Chapter 13: Descent Into Controversy

"You always claim that you're the oldest, most experienced, and professional legal firm, but you don't bother to say we don't think ... we just bill. None of you, not one of you, said Maxwell would pay off his loan and fight." Mr. Arnold's temper exploded as he mercilessly berated the attorneys who had gathered in his office. "He's got to go! Start writing a news release for the Securities Department to use. See to it that it's printed on the front page of The Daily newspaper this weekend." he shouted. Arnold was filled with fury and rage. He needed Graydon Maxwell out of his way and would do whatever was necessary to make it happen. Feeling humiliated, the legal team looked down and cowered like little children.

The leading lawyer finally uttered, "We tried, sir. But no one had expected or thought he could find another lender."

"Stop talking and go get the news release written." Mr. Arnold demanded as he pointed toward the door.

***

Meanwhile, Graydon remained undeterred in his work. He had always left the house before 6:00 A.M. each workday to accomplish all he needed to so he could leave the office ahead of the afternoon traffic rush. Having family time was a top priority for Graydon and Sophie, so he tried to be home as much as possible before supper. The usual evening routine included play, dinner and conversation, more play, reading, and bedtime. With the girls tucked in and dreaming sweetly, the couple enjoyed talking to each other about their day. Graydon usually shared an entertaining story about the office while Sophie informed him of the girls' activities and progress at school.

On Wednesday evening, he began their conversation by asking, "Did you know the State Securities Department can announce an investigation without giving the one being investigated any notice, information, or chance to respond?"

"What are you talking about? I know a little about FINRA and the SEC, but not about a State Securities Department." Sophie expressed her bewilderment.

"On Monday afternoon, the SSD posted a notice on their website announcing they are investigating the securities firm. Frustratingly, I didn't hear a word from the department and only found out about the investigation on Tuesday because our new intern heard the news from a friend. They don't have any jurisdiction over the ETFs or our mortgage activities. I called Joe immediately, so he reached out to them and was told the investigator was unavailable until next week. At the same time, Jay Willard called, came in to meet with me this morning, and asked me to resign, to which I said, I'm not in default, and I'm going to pay you off."

"Mr. Willard called, came to see you, and asked you to resign?" She could not believe what she heard. It was utterly shocking. "That makes no sense. Jay has known you for many years. He's always respected and admired you, and we've made our loan payments diligently. I don't understand why he would ask you to resign. What's really going on?" she asked.

"I haven't done anything wrong, so I have no earthly idea as to what's being discussed and made up." Sophie's expression became soft as she let out a gentle sigh and looked at him with a tilted head. Her eyes filled with compassion for him.

"I know you haven't and never would do anything illegal. The timing of this is very suspect; we just got back from New York, and this happened. Who's mad at us?" she questioned.

"Well, no way it's us; it's me they are mad at," Graydon said, "I'm still trying to solve the mystery," he continued as Sophie listened intently. "And, until I know what the investigation is about, I'm unsure what to do. One of my first thoughts was that Mr. Willard would be at risk. I decided to make arrangements to move the loan before he called, so that was definitely inspired."

"We've always stayed on the right path forward. We're equally yoked. We'll figure out what to do. How'd you move the loan so quickly?" she asked.

"We're way ahead of the repayment schedule, and the ETFs are throwing off more income as they've increased in size. I've talked to several private equity funds since we rang the bell and expect significant growth after this month's performance is released. We have an exceptional story and are building a better one." Graydon reported.

***

"You're calling me on Friday at 4:55 P.M., and I know your deadline for printing is in 5 minutes. You say that you just 'happened' to see a notice on their website and want my comment? You don't want my comment; your article has already been written by someone who knows how to make false accusations. So, I'll say no comment other than the sun will come up tomorrow." he hung up and frowned.

The week before the NYSE bell rang, the newspaper's business writer and editor had been in Graydon's office to discuss InnovateX's success as they planned to print a feature article. As their conversation neared the end, they veered off course as both expressed their interest in joining the firm as an in-house media and public relations team.

Graydon was intrigued by their carefully thought-out pitch as he knew the range and value of proper media relations. He told them he would consider it and thanked them for their time and interest. After they left, he immediately searched for their most recent articles to gauge their professionalism and styles. When he discussed it with Sophie that evening, they both decided they had more questions than answers and agreed to put this idea on hold. Nonetheless, they both recognized the impact of how the ever-expanding world of communication was now occurring at nearly instant speed and that most people believe what they read, whether it's true or not.

****

"Who was that?" Sophie asked, worried.

"The business writer for The Daily," he replied in a visibly annoyed manner. "Said he just 'happened' to see the notice. Can you believe that just days ago, he wanted us to hire him, and now he's ready to print an article that's likely to destroy us? We had better call our parents before they see or hear about it and let them know a tall tale is about to be told. They'll be shocked."

The next afternoon, their children were in the driveway drawing pictures of their favorite flowers with sidewalk chalk. Graydon and Sophie were busy tidying up the kitchen when their daughters appeared, visibly upset. The youngest was in tears, while the oldest reported with a puzzled look that as a group of neighborhood children rode by, one stopped and said, "My dad told my mom that your daddy is going to jail soon! Is that true?" Alarmed, Sophie and Graydon looked at each other with dismay, realizing the story was out. "They even showed us this," she said, handing a newspaper to them and pointing to an article. It had a picture of Graydon in front of the NYSE after the bell-ringing ceremony. The headline read, "Maxwell Securities is the Target of Review."

Graydon felt as if his soul had completely washed out of his body as he read the scathing article, which dominated the first page of the business section. The article ended with a quote from the head administrator of the State Department of Securities, "Because of their high profile, we need to inform the public."

Sophie successfully masked her initial shock to protect their children, but as she read the article, she felt bewildered, afraid, and angry. While she fought to hold back her tears, she swiftly embraced both girls, "Truth wins, girls. Always remember that, and don't worry about what people say. All that matters is that you both know Mommy and Daddy love you very much and we will always protect you."

"So, Daddy is not going to jail?" they both asked.

"Absolutely not!" Graydon replied. "Girls, remember the verse we talked about yesterday, God hates liars? Sometimes, people don't know the truth; they believe what they read or hear and don't seek to find out the truth themselves. Just know we always, always, always tell and seek the truth." They held hands, bowed their heads, and prayed together.

***

The print headlines served their purpose, damaging Maxwell's reputation beyond repair. Most folks who read the article gleefully assumed that the printed words were true, in large part, to soothe the pangs of their jealousy over Maxwell's impeccable character and success. Many of their closest friends offered support with kind words of encouragement. There were others, including family members, who were suspicious and distanced themselves from the Maxwells.

Graydon was a very kind and generous employer, starting each week with an all-hands meeting featuring a catered breakfast. The meeting encouraged camaraderie and boosted morale for the week's tasks. Of course, this Monday was different. Graydon sensed heaviness as everyone gathered around the trading desk. "I'm sure you've all read the article in Saturday's newspaper. As you all can imagine, it was a total shock to my wife and I as none of it is true. I assume you all were surprised, too, and no doubt have concerns about the future of the company. The slanderous allegations are baseless and designed to cause damage, which we pray will not be irreparable. We are taking the necessary measures to rectify what has happened and move forward with continued success. However, If you believe it's in your and your customers' best interest to leave and move to another brokerage, we will not impede you. I plan to be in my office all day, so feel free to ask questions, and I will answer them as best I can at this point." Without looking back at their reaction, he returned to his office and called Joe.

"Why can't we get any information from the State Securities Department? I cannot believe they can launch this investigation without notifying me," he asked once again.

"Because they are a quasi-government agency, meaning they receive support from the State but are managed independently. They can and do make up rules to protect and serve their interests. You'll hear from me the moment after I speak to the investigator." Joe informed him.

The next afternoon, eight days after the website posting, Joe called. "I spoke with the lead investigator for less than a minute." He updated. "She said they have questions about a recent municipal underwriting. Apparently, they are 'suspicious' about the truthfulness of certain materials. They'll be sending you a letter asking for copies of files." Graydon had never imagined a situation like this. After he left the office, the letter came in via e-mail. After he arrived home, he opened it and immediately forwarded it to Joe, who called a few minutes later and said, "I have never seen or heard of an information request this lengthy. I doubt five people working all day in the files and at the copier can get this done."

"All under the cover of a 'legal verification' Rule that they created and has no bearing or meaning in a real court, right?" Graydon asked.

Joe reluctantly agreed with a weak "Uh huh. This is clearly a message sent to pressure you not to defend yourself. This is how they kill off people and firms. Make the burden and costs so high they can't survive. Then the agency never has to present and prove the allegations."

"Who are these people?" Graydon continued

"Don't quote me. They're folks who couldn't make it elsewhere and have sold their souls to the powers to be in exchange for 9-5 Monday to Friday employment with excellent benefits that don't end with retirement," he said in a disgusted and dismal tone.

"What's with the form Sophie and I have to sign giving them authorization to request and receive the last three years of our banking records?" Graydon asked regarding one of the required documents.

"They lobbied the legislature a few years ago for expanded powers. You do understand people outside their agency will be given copies of what they gather, don't you?" Joe rhetorically questioned him.

"No. I am completely ignorant of who they are and what they do. I never had a class or work session on 'Fear the Powers of the Regulators.' I didn't do anything wrong! I never expected to become a victim, which I'm now learning defines their word 'target.'" Graydon cynically commented.

"I understand, but at the moment, I don't know how you can solve it." Joe apologetically responded.

"Well, I'm going to go through this believing a few loyal clients will stay with me," Graydon said confidently. He was sure that he had developed relationships in the market that were not going to leave his side.

***

"How is he still operating?" Mr. Arnold asked the attorneys, who, once again, stood before him three months after the announcement.

"We don't know other than he's made a lot of money for the customers that followed his recommendations, and they must not believe in what they've heard or read. We do know the number of customers and the assets under management for the securities firm have dropped dramatically." the leading attorney said.

"And yet, the ETFs are still alive. Which one of you works with Toby Schools?" Arnold asked.

The eldest nodded as he spoke, "I have for over 30 years."

"Write up a FINRA Arbitration Complaint for them off their recent $30 Million underwriting done with the securities firm. The State can use it to formalize their investigation and announce their allegations. There is no way Maxwell will survive another headline and those two battles." Arnold instructed him.

"I thought you wanted the securities firm." One of the junior associates spoke and immediately regretted speaking as he saw Arnold's expression.

"That was only if he walked away without any headlines. All I want now is the ETFs liquidated and our shares back in the marketplace!" Arnold said harshly.

***

Three weeks later, Graydon walked into Joe's office with a FedEx envelope in hand. "From FINRA, an Arbitration Notice for the Toby Schools underwriting." He held up the envelope high to show it. Then he read it out loud: "Conducted inadequate due diligence and, thus, failed to form a reasonable basis for believing the truthfulness of certain material representations in official statements. Oh, and it gets better," he continued, "Offered and sold municipal securities based on materially misleading disclosure documents, a violation of antifraud provisions of the federal securities laws." He looked up from the letter at Joe and then rolled his eyes, mockingly affirming, "You're looking at a dead man walking. Antifraud is their firing squad word." They both were quiet. "I don't know how I am supposed to react anymore, Joe."

"Do not worry, my friend. Your life has much more to it than this. You will recover and move forward." Joe tried his best to sound reassuring.

Two weeks later, the State's formal Notice of Opportunity for Hearing with Enforcement Division Recommendation arrived via snail mail. Graydon was not surprised to read a near-verbatim copy of the FINRA Arbitration claims.

"The State didn't even try to veer off FINRA's path," Graydon said to Joe. "I don't believe they had anything to investigate when they announced. That's why we didn't receive a notification before the website posting. Why the investigation? Why didn't we get this before today? They created theirs' off FINRA's back." He articulated.

"That now seems likely. The question is, how do you fight and survive? Do you want to fight?" Joe was concerned because he knew a battle with such powerful forces would be impractical.

"I didn't do anything wrong. I was raised with the belief you stand on top of the mountain and shout if you're wrongly accused, that truth wins." Graydon was firm in his belief.

"I get that, but the lies remain. Why don't you think about it overnight? Let's visit again in the morning." he suggested.

"No. No thought is required other than dot the i's and cross the t's. Do everything you have to do to defend my credibility. There's a greater point to be made. We've enjoyed success, but integrity matters far more. I can't roll over to false fraud charges. I know who my source is." Graydon held his head high.

Another month passed, and a third strike was delivered. Securities firms utilize clearing firms to process their transactions. Maxwell Securities utilized the industry leader, Global Financial Solutions. Their letter simply stated, "Without cause, we have decided to terminate your clearing agreement." Joe reported back that he was told they were concerned about the potential for the arbitration claim to result in a large award and render Maxwell insolvent. This was the last blow.

Graydon accepted reality. The ETFs had not gained any additional investors given the name association with the securities firm's 'antifraud' allegations. They would have to be liquidated. The Securities firm could not operate without a Clearing Agreement. He told Joe to file the necessary forms and paperwork. Both the ETFs and Maxwell Securities were forced to close 60 days later.

The accusations had come swiftly and with brutal force, like a storm crashing against Graydon's world. He'd been so careful, so dedicated to building their company into something respected and innovative, but now all of it seemed to hang in the balance. Sitting in his home office, Graydon gripped the edge of his desk, staring at the articles spreading across financial news sites. "I have to fight them now!" he uttered.

Sophie sat across from him, her expression resolute. She'd always been his rock, the one person who could steady him in a crisis. As much as she wanted to retaliate by suing the newspaper for defaming her husband, she wasn't sure it would be worth the toll it would take to fight a losing battle. Perhaps it would be best to rest in the fact that God knows the real story. After all, that's what matters most.

"Graydon, I understand why you want to fight back. I believe it's important to stand up for truth and justice. But I'm not confident it's possible to win even if you fight off the false charges," she said with concern. "A victory after years still leaves a stain. Every Google search will point to these accusations. The articles are written in a way that defamation charges will never win. The attorneys will charge exorbitant fees for as long as they can be paid, never completing their work."

Graydon looked at her, and his heart sank. He knew she was right. The damage would be done even if they managed to clear his name. The other side would continue to request volumes of files and information, which would be invasive and completely unnecessary but within their right to ask. They'd file endless motions, dragging the process out, constantly extending the timeline. Other agencies would be encouraged to pile on, increasing the burden on them individually and on their company.

Sophie continued in a steady but firm voice. "Our children will hear and see stories that we are 'bad guys.' The children's well-being is a target the accusers will use to batter us. All the business glory and prestige have never mattered to me. I know we don't need any of it to be happy. And I know you'll figure out how to succeed again in a way that others can't derail."

Graydon sighed. He'd spent all his time up to this point building his career, sacrificing time and energy to create something he could be proud of. But Sophie's right! He looked at her; her eyes were filled with love and understanding. He knew he could not put their family through this.

"The Sun will come up tomorrow, right?" she said, smiling gently. "I know the truth will win in the end, but sometimes, especially when you're persecuted for righteousness's sake, it's best to walk away from the fight."

Graydon nodded in agreement. They focused their attention on moving forward as quickly as possible. They sold their home and moved to a quiet mountain-top acreage in a different state where they could rebuild their lives without the constant scrutiny of the business and media world. Graydon continued to manage their holdings and investments, focusing on what truly mattered: their family and their future.

Shortly after relocating, several former clients and friends contacted Graydon. They constantly reminded him that he was not abandoned and that "truth wins." His devoted clients assured Graydon of their trust as they hired him to help manage their assets as before.

On the first Thanksgiving morning in their new home, while their parents took over the kitchen and entertained the grandchildren, Graydon and Sophie sipped their coffee on the porch overlooking the tranquil mountain landscape. The breathtaking view reminded them of God's faithful provision, and they both knew the next chapter of their lives would unfold with blessings that would far exceed the brokenness they left behind.